UNOFFICIAL DETECTIVE

HALF-WIZARD THORDRIC BOOK 1

KATHRYN WELLS

To ma and pa, for believing.

INTRODUCING THORDRIC

'I'm telling you, Inspector, he's a sensible young man.'

Thordric heard Inspector Jimmson sigh. His mother had been in the inspector's office for over an hour, trying to negotiate with him to get Thordric a job at the station. 'I don't doubt it, Maggie, but there's no denying what he is.' The inspector lowered his voice, so that Thordric had to strain to hear. 'He's a *half*-wizard, for Spell's sake. If it ever got out that one of his kind was working here—'

'*His* kind? Inspector, I *assure* you that particular part of him is completely under control,' his mother retorted.

'Maggie, Maggie. Think of what you're asking me to do here. You know you're the best pathologist I could possibly hope for, and I wouldn't want to do anything to upset you, but the reputation of the stationhouse...' There was silence for a moment. 'I just can't let the boy work here.'

Thordric heard one of the chairs scrape back. 'Then you're not the man I thought you were,' his mother said. The door to the office opened, and she walked out, holding her head high and clacking her high heels with proud deliberation. 'Come on Thordric, let's go home.'

Thordric got up, a mix of relief and disappointment filling his stomach. They turned to go, but then the office door opened again. The inspector walked out, eyeing Thordric up with a twitch of his bushy moustache. Thordric tried not to gulp under the inspector's scrutinising gaze.

'He's hired,' the inspector said abruptly. 'Starts work tomorrow morning, seven-thirty on the dot. Don't let him be late, Maggie.'

'Thank you, Inspector,' his mother said. Thordric thought he saw a smile flicker across her lips.

Later that day, she took him to the tailor to get his uniform measured. As he was only to be the inspector's runner, he didn't need the full constabulary uniform.

'Good thing, too,' the tailor said, lifting a measuring tape up to Thordric's chest. 'I don't believe I have any small enough. No, indeed, it will have to be a plain jacket, though in a boy's size, I think.'

He took the measurement, scribbling the number down in his leather-bound notebook. Thordric craned his neck to try and see what it was, but the tailor held his hand up. 'Please, sir, you shouldn't trouble yourself with the details. Leave that to me.' He turned to Thordric's mother then, and dropped his voice slightly. 'Are you sure he's fourteen? He looks to be no more than twelve at the most, if I am honest, Ma'am.'

'I'm fourteen and a half,' Thordric said indignantly. The tailor smiled faintly and carried on taking measurements.

A few hours later, Thordric came out with his new uniform in hand, ready to head home, but his mother caught his arm and took him to the barber shop instead. 'What are we doing here?' he said, standing in front of the entrance, looking at the red and white pole spinning around and around on the wall.

'You'll want to look smart tomorrow, won't you, dear?' she said mildly.

The barber found fault with him too, complaining that Thordric's hair was in such bad condition that he couldn't possibly cut it into any of the regular constabulary styles (though it was not for lack of trying). After three hours, growing increasingly hot and flustered, he'd declared the only thing he could do to make Thordric look smart was to shave it all off.

'Oh, do stop fussing, Thordric,' his mother said after the deed had been done. 'If that's what the good barber thought best to do, then it was best.'

'But...but, it's so short. All I have is stubble. Everyone is going to laugh at me.'

'Nonsense,' she chided. 'It looks very smart. I'm sure that no one will say anything bad.'

Unfortunately for Thordric, she couldn't have been more wrong.

At seven-thirty sharp she dropped him at the front desk, and there he stood in his new clothes with his bald head reflecting the morning light. The constable at the desk took one look at him and threw his head back, laughing so much that it brought all the other constables out to have a look. Some of them sniggered or tried to stifle their snorts, but most laughed as hard as the desk constable.

'Look at him,' Thordric heard one of them whisper. 'He's nothing more than a string bean. What possessed the inspector to hire him?'

All the commotion brought the inspector looming around the corner, with his face resembling the very storm cloud that had drenched the whole town the night before. All the constables took one look at him and quailed, fleeing back to their desks and burying their heads in paperwork.

'There you are, er, Thorbid,' he said, his eyes marking every detail of Thordric's clothes and physique. 'Hardly constabulary material, but I suppose you'll do. Come along.'

'Inspector?' Thordric said with a squeak. 'It's Thordric, not Thorbid.'

'Quiet now, Throbay. Follow me.'

Thordric followed meekly, past the constables' desks and into the inspector's office. It was a neat room, furnished with dark wooden bookcases and a wooden desk. There wasn't a single speck of dust to be seen. 'Now,' the inspector said, sitting down in his vast leather chair. 'I'm sure your mother has explained your duties to you already. Still, I see no reason not to remind you again. Your role here is to be my runner. You will do as I say, fetch things and bring them back at my command, post any letters that need to be posted, and make tea whenever I feel the need for it. You will not, I repeat: *NOT*, speak to any of the constables, and are absolutely forbidden to assist them with any policing duties. And if anyone finds out that you're a *you know what*, then you'll be out of here faster than your own feet can carry you. Understand?' he said, stroking his thick bushy moustache.

'Yes, sir,' Thordric said, his voice breaking awkwardly.

'Inspector,' the inspector said.

'What, sir?'

'You say, "Yes, Inspector".'

'Oh, of course,' Thordric mumbled. 'Yes, Inspector.'

'Good,' the inspector said cheerfully. 'Go make me a cup of tea and fetch me some Jaffa cakes.'

. . .

Thordric spent the rest of the morning bringing the inspector large cups of tea ('No, no, Thorble, *two* sugars and not so much milk!'), passing messages back and forth throughout the station house and pretending not to be there whenever one of the constables walked past. He barely had time to visit his mother when she broke for lunch, and when he did, he found she had no sympathy for him.

'I don't know what you expected, Thordric. You knew life at the station was going to be hard.'

'Yes, but not *this* hard.'

'Oh, Thordric. You're not a baby anymore, you're almost fifteen.'

'I know,' he said, hanging his head. 'But why couldn't I have gone to the academy like all my friends?'

His mother breathed out slowly. 'You know perfectly well why. This is the only way I could guarantee you a future.' She took a sip of her coffee, a special blend developed by the Wizard Council to help re-energise and focus the mind. 'You ought to be getting back now, the inspector will be asking for you.'

'But I haven't even had anything to eat yet!'

'You should have thought of that before you came running to me. You shouldn't come here while you're working. I'm perfectly fine.'

'Yes, mother,' Thordric said, slinking off back to the station.

The inspector was waiting for him when he got there, his moustache curling up into his nostrils as he glared at Thordric. 'Thormble! Where were you? I've been looking all over for you! Go and fetch me a copy of the local newspaper.'

'Yes, Inspector,' he said, walking as quickly as possible without making it look as though he was running away.

It was raining when he got outside; the new rainbow colours that were now so popular with other adolescents his age. He looked up and saw them sprinkling the powder into the rain from the rooftop of the library, and as it mixed, the drops turned into bright reds, oranges and pinks.

He would've loved to have joined them, to have a go as they did, but he was forbidden to touch anything the Wizard Council had produced. His mother told him that if he did, it would be incredibly dangerous. Anything could happen if it mixed with his rogue half-wizard magic. His mother had made sure that he'd grown up knowing the risk, telling him stories of half-wizards who had tried to experiment and ended up losing various limbs, turning themselves into animals, or in the case of a particularly unfortunate one, a pumpkin.

It'd scared him when he was younger, but now he wished he could prove everyone wrong about it. He wanted to show them that half-wizard magic wasn't always harmful, that *his* magic wasn't harmful, but his mother would never forgive him if he tried. She had wanted to bring him up as a respectable young man, and to ignore his wizard side, forget it was there. But he couldn't. It took over his dreams, willing him to try things out, and once or twice had even taken control of his body.

He remembered one time when he had been at junior school; one of the older boys had found out what he was and decided to tell everyone. Thordric had been so upset that he'd clapped his hands together and made everyone, including his teachers, forget all about it. Unfortunately, the boy who had started it was hit by Thordric's powers directly, resulting in him losing his entire memory.

The school wrote it off as a freak accident, but Thordric's mother had known better. She'd sat him down and asked, kindly, what really happened. He told her, knowing that it'd been wrong, but that he simply hadn't been able to control it.

She'd comforted him, but said if anything like it happened again, he was to tell her straight away.

Sadly, despite his good intentions, *she* had been the victim of his power's next attack, while telling him off for making a mess of her study. Unbidden, he'd stamped his foot and sent her off on a completely different train of thought, and since she hadn't seemed to notice, he thought it better to simply let her carry on and not tell her what had happened.

Thinking back to those days when he was younger, he wondered ruefully how different it would have been had he been born normal. One of the coloured raindrops landed on his nose, and with a shake of his head he remembered that he was supposed to be on his way to the newspaper stand to get the inspector a copy of the *Jard Town Gazette*.

He quickened his pace, but when he got there, he found that they'd sold out. The vendor told him that he might try the stand across the town, and so he had to race over there to fetch one. *That* vendor was on his last copy, and sold it to Thordric for double what it was worth, seeing how much of a hurry he was in.

'Oi, you're not the inspector's usual fry, are you?'

'No, sir,' Thordric said, making to dash away.

'When did you start then?' the vendor continued.

'Er, today, actually,' Thordric said, and disappeared before he could be asked anything else.

He ran back to the station, making record time, and was so impressed with himself that he didn't see the inspector standing in the doorway of his office. The resulting crash echoed throughout the building, and once again all the constables dashed to have a look. They found the inspector lying on the floor with his head in the waste paper basket. Thordric had bounced off the inspector's considerable bulk to land over by the bookcase, with a copy of *The Detective's Handbook* open on

7

his head. His eyes were vacant as the constables rushed past him to see to the inspector.

'Inspector?' one said, daring to shake him slightly. 'Inspector Jimmson, can you hear me?'

The inspector mumbled something incoherent. The constable rounded on Thordric. 'Look at what you've done, small fry! Didn't anyone tell you not to run in the station?'

Thordric didn't hear him. The constable slapped him hard. 'I'm talking to you, small fry.'

'Wh-what?' Thordric said, his eyes starting to focus. He saw the inspector, semi-conscious and unmoving. 'Blimey, what happened to the inspector?' he said. The constable hit him again.

'Ouch,' he said. 'What was that for?'

'Oh, never mind,' the constable said, giving up. He turned to one of the other constables. 'Fred, see if you can get this twit home. He won't be any use to anyone for the rest of today. I'll deal with the inspector.'

The constable known as Fred grabbed Thordric and dragged him out of the station to the morgue, where the constable felt it was his duty to inform his mother of what had happened. She was less than impressed.

'Thordric Manfred Smallchance! How could you? And on your first day, too!' She threw her hands up in the air, quite forgetting that they were covered with blood from the latest poor soul she was performing a post-mortem on. 'Take him home, constable, and lock the door so that he can't cause any more trouble.'

2

THE INSPECTOR'S SISTER

Thordric woke to the sound of his mother rapping on his bedroom door. 'Thordric. Thordric! It's time to get up!'

He furrowed his brow, his eyes too heavy to open.

'Thordric, get up,' his mother continued, still knocking on the door. 'You must go and apologise to the inspector.' He heard her sigh and turn away.

At first it didn't register with him what she had said, but then he remembered. He had fallen into the inspector and left him barely conscious. Swallowing the sudden lump in his throat, he scrambled out of bed and fumbled on his clothes before bolting downstairs.

His mother was waiting for him when he got there. He thought she looked especially pretty today. Her dark, wavy hair was loose about her shoulders and she wearing her crimson heels, but he knew that if he told her, she would see it as buttering her up. That was one thing she hated.

'I hope you realise the seriousness of the damage you did yesterday,' she said crisply. 'When the poor Inspector finally got his wits back, I had to plead with him for hours to give you another chance.'

'I...' Thordric began, but found he had no words.

'I expect you never to make a mistake or cause trouble like that again. Had the inspector not been the type to demonstrate perfect chivalry, then it may have cost my job as well as yours. As it is, he values my friendship very deeply and has agreed to overlook the matter. But only this once.'

'I understand, mother. I won't do it again, I promise.'

'Well, then,' she said. 'Off you go, and don't forget to make his tea exactly how he likes it. And don't complain about the constables. You deserve their crude remarks at the moment.' Thordric had to agree. How could he have messed up his first day so badly? Not even the other half-wizards he had read about had *that* much bad luck.

He sped to the station, arriving even before the inspector, and had a steaming mug of tea and a plate of Jaffa cakes ready for him. When the inspector finally walked in, he said nothing, choosing to ignore Thordric completely. Halfway through his fifth Jaffa cake, however, he decided to speak up. 'I never want to speak of what happened yesterday. It was a normal day like any other. Understood?'

'Yes, Inspector,' Thordric said, bowing his head.

The inspector wiped the crumbs off his moustache. 'Here,' he said, thrusting a piece of paper at Thordric. 'Go to the dry cleaners on Warn Street and show them that. They will give you my sister's dry cleaning, which you will then proceed to drop off at her house. Here is her address.' He scribbled on another bit of paper and handed it to Thordric. 'You are then to ask her if any chores need attending to, and if she so wishes, you shall do them for her.'

'But...' Thordric protested, but stopped at the inspector's glare.

'You are then to go to the bank and give them this,' he continued, giving Thordric yet another piece of paper. 'And then you are to get the *Jard Town Gazette*. Make sure it is today's copy, and not a leftover from yesterday. Is that clear?'

'Yes, Inspector,' Thordric said, trying to keep his voice sounding positive.

'Remember Thormble, *no mistakes.*'

Thordric left the office with as much grace as he could muster. He looked at the notes in his hand, trying to remember which was which. The inspector's sister's address was easy to recognise, but the notes for the dry cleaners and bank were both numbers. Each had been written in a great long line with no breaks, and there was nothing to differentiate between them. He gulped.

He reached the dry cleaners quickly, sweating slightly from the heat of the shop. 'Yes, sir?' the woman at the desk said without even looking at him. She was reading a magazine, intent on an article about using the Wizard Council's new spell powder to get rid of fleas and bugs from the home. She nodded as she read, and Thordric grumbled under his breath. He hated the Wizard Council. True, they did make a lot of fun things, like their new Rainbow range, but that was only the lower part of the council. High Wizard Kalljard would never have had anything to do with them; he was far too important for that trivial stuff. *He* was the one who Thordric really disliked, for it was he who had spread such hate for half-wizards, despite the rumours that he had fathered a half-wizard himself.

Before Kalljard had come to power, half-wizards had been trusted as much as everyone else, and people had often gone to them for help when they couldn't afford the prices of a full wizard. But that had been over a thousand years ago now, for it was Kalljard's discovery of everlasting youth that had allowed him to form the council and take charge of it. No one had successfully got him to share his secrets of everlasting youth, but he had developed a potion that allowed the elderly to look and feel young in the last days of their lives.

Full wizards were actually quite rare, only a handful were born each year. Each full wizard was born into a family with no previous magic in it and it was said that the powers they had came from all the potential magic that the family had within their bloodline. To keep their powers pure, full wizards were not allowed to marry. Of course, if they all obeyed that rule then there wouldn't be any half-wizards.

The woman finished her article and looked up, frowning slightly as she saw his stubbly head. 'I have to pick up the inspector's sister's dry cleaning,' he said, the words tripping out of his mouth.

She raised her eyebrows at him. 'Do you have the inspector's pass code?'

'Yes, I...'

He looked at the two notes, grimacing. It was impossible to tell which one it was. Shrugging, he chose one at random and handed it to her. She looked at it and checked it against her list. 'That is indeed the inspector's pass code,' she said, the surprise showing in her voice. 'One moment, sir.'

She went into the backroom, and appeared a moment later with a huge stack of clothes. 'Here you are, sir. Tell the inspector that we thank him for his custom.' She handed them to him, making his knees buckle slightly. Easing a smile onto his face, he thanked her and inched out the door. How could anyone own so many clothes?

Once out in the street, he found a postbox to lean against while he fished the address out of his pocket. He read it and cursed: 52, Rosemary Lane. That was on the other side of town. He could almost feel the ache in his muscles at the very idea of it.

By the time he reached the cherry-red front door which was surrounded by honeysuckle, his feet felt like they were covered in blisters, and he was sweating profusely. Not wanting to offend the lady, he quickly straightened his uniform, shifting the pile of clothes to one arm. The door opened before he could even knock, and a woman stood inches from his nose. Her hair was in a bun so tight that it gave her a slight facelift. Thordric felt his knees begin to buckle again.

'And who might you be?' she said.

'I'm Thordric, ma'am. The inspector sent me to deliver your dry cleaning.'

She pursed her lips. 'Very well, then. Bring it in and leave it on the banister. Quickly, boy!'

He did as he was told, feeling her eyes bore into his back.

'Well, why are you still here?' she said.

'The inspector asked me to ask you if you had any chores that need doing, ma'am, and if so to do them for you.'

'It seems that my brother has finally developed some manners then. Come along, boy, and let us see what you can do.' Thordric thought he saw a smile flicker across her lips, but it was gone too quickly for him to be sure.

She led him to the kitchen. It was a large room, with a dark stove at its heart, and Thordric caught the most wonderful smell coming from it. It was roast chicken and potatoes, and his stomach groaned audibly. The inspector's sister took no notice. Instead, she dived into one of the oversized cupboards and produced a battered copper kettle.

'I want you to fix this kettle,' she said, handing it to him.

He looked at it doubtfully, noticing several large dents and a gash in the side. 'I'll try, ma'am, but I don't pretend to have the skills to do it.'

'Hogwash, boy!' she scoffed. 'Use your magic.'

Thordric gaped. 'You know that I'm a half-wizard?'

She laughed. 'Don't be silly, boy. I can smell your powers from half a mile away, they're so strong. In fact, I thought you were from the Wizard Council, which was why I was so concerned when you turned up on my doorstep.'

'What do you mean, you can *smell* my powers?' he said, his voice breaking.

'Forgive me, smell is perhaps the wrong word. Sense is more accurate, I suppose. It was my late husband who taught me how, you see. He was a half-wizard too.'

'He was?'

'Yes. Come and sit down, now I know that you're safe.' She led him into the conservatory and made him sit on a light-cream wicker sofa.

'You don't trust the Wizard Council, then?' he asked.

'Of course not,' she said, failing to keep the contempt out of her voice. 'Greedy, soulless lot they are. Drove my poor husband to his death.'

'How?' he said, before he could stop himself.

She sighed. 'I suppose you've heard the stories of half-wizards trying to prove themselves? Well, my husband was the same. He created many spells equally as good as any that come from the Wizard Council. He developed potions too, most of them more effective that any the council make. He had an argument with a full wizard about it all, right out in the street. He came home raging, so I suggested that he go for a walk along the quieter lanes to clear his head. He didn't want to, but he went anyway. He didn't come home that night.' She dabbed her eyes with a handkerchief. 'They found his body the next morning, a deep purple colour. My brother, who had only just been made Inspector back then, kept it all quiet for me so I wouldn't have the papers knocking on my door. He said that the pathologist believed he had been trying a spell and like most half-wizards had met his downfall in doing so.'

14

'I'm sorry,' Thordric said, awkwardly patting her on the shoulder.

'Thank you, boy. It was a long time ago,' she said, sniffing and sitting up. 'Right. Now I need to find out more about you. Who was your father?'

'Mother never told me. All she said was that he was a wizard.'

'Presumably on the council, then?'

'I guess so. Aren't all full wizards on the council?'

'No. There are those who disagree with what the council does, and refuse to have anything to do with it. They are shunned as much as you half-wizards though, so many don't advertise their powers.'

'Oh. I see,' Thordric replied, shifting on the sofa. 'Wh-why is it you want to know about me, ma'am?'

'Please, call me Lizzie,' she said, waving a hand. 'The truth is I want to help you. If you have even half the power that I think you have, then you are capable of doing great things, not to mention fixing my poor kettle.' She laughed and let down her bun slightly, taking away the hardness from her face. 'Now, how much magic can you do at the moment?'

Thordric felt deflated. 'None,' he said.

'Oh, come now, surely you've done something?' Lizzie said.

'Well, I may have accidently caused some people to lose their memory or forget what they were saying. I've never done anything on purpose though. Mother said that it's too dangerous.'

'Tosh!' Lizzie said. 'Well, I've certainly got my work cut out with you.' She stood up and took him out into the garden, where she stood him in front of a dead tree stump. It was raining heavily, but she didn't seem to notice.

'Now,' she said, her voice taking on its crispness again. 'The first thing you have to do is learn how to focus your powers.'

She stretched out her arm, pointing with index finger. 'I want you to focus all of your attention on this tree stump, and when you think you've got it, you are to paint a red dot right in the middle of it.'

'But I don't have any paint,' he said.

The look she gave him made the stubble on his head frizzle. 'Do it with your powers, boy!'

'But I don't know how,' he complained.

Lizzie huffed. 'Simply focus and *think* about painting it like you would manually.'

During the next hour, while water had filled up his boots and now trickled over the tops, Thordric had managed to paint dots all over the garden fence, the shed and the bushes, but not one had landed on the tree stump.

Lizzie had watched him tirelessly. 'Where are you aiming for, boy? The target is in front of you, not behind!' she said. 'Focus. Feel the power within you and push it forwards.'

At one point he turned around to tell her that it simply wasn't possible, but caught her square in the head with a red dot of paint. Instead of being angry with him she fell about laughing. 'I do believe that it's time for a spot of tea.'

Gathering up her now soaked skirts, she sat him in the kitchen to contemplate the battered kettle. 'What makes you think I can fix this when I can't even put a dot on a tree stump?' he asked in dismay.

'Do you, or do you not, want tea?' she asked, arching an eyebrow high into her hair.

'Yes, I do.'

'Then you will fix the kettle. It's as simple as that.' She got up and bustled around the kitchen. 'Oh, and don't be too long with it, I want the tea ready by the time I finish baking this cake. And you'll want to get to the bank before it closes,' she said. He jumped. How did she know that he needed to go there?

He shrugged and turned back to the kettle. It sat there, his reflection staring back at him, distorted and grubby on its lacklustre surface. He sighed and clapped his hands together, hoping the motion would give him some hint of an idea how fix it. It didn't.

He decided to work on the dents first. Perhaps if he pushed at them from the inside, it would shift the metal back out again. The first few tries he missed, and had used such a force that it sent him sailing across the kitchen and back out into the conservatory.

Lizzie smiled, and said only, 'Keep trying, boy.'

Slowly, his aim improved, and he managed to fix two of the bigger dents. 'Now try and fix that gash,' Lizzie said over his shoulder. 'The cake is almost ready.'

By this time, Thordric was sweating almost as much as he had been while carrying her clothes. He couldn't believe how much energy it took to use his powers. Did all wizards struggle like this? Or was it solely half-wizards?

He wiped the sweat away from his forehead, and to give himself a better idea of what the gash was like, he put his hands on it. As soon as he did, he felt the most curious sensation. He could feel the kettle, not just how it was now in his hands, but how it had been when it was first made. Smooth and perfectly round. Focusing on this, he willed it to be like that again, closing his eyes tightly.

Lizzie clapped loudly. 'Open your eyes, boy,' she said. He could hear the smile in her voice, and as he opened his eyes again, he saw why. He'd done it. The kettle was brand new again. No dents or gashes at all, nor even a hint of where they had been.

He jumped up out of his seat, with a grin so wide that it barely fit his face, and ran back outside into the rain, painting a red dot on the tree stump without even thinking about it. He felt so light, and so *free*. He had used magic – his magic – and it'd worked. He danced around the garden, swinging the kettle about as if it were his partner, only stopping when Lizzie caught him by the arm and dragged him back inside.

'Steady yourself, boy. I need that,' she said, pulling the kettle away from him.

'Did you see, Lizzie? Did you see me put the paint on the tree stump?' he laughed. His body shook with so much excitement and nervous energy that he wobbled like a jelly. Lizzie steered him into a chair by the table.

'I did, boy, I did. But don't think that you've finished your training yet. You've an awful lot more to learn.' She planted a cup of tea beside him and a slice of cake so large that it filled the plate. 'Eat that. It'll give you your energy back.'

A few mouthfuls later he was calm again. 'How will I finish my training?' he said. 'The inspector will want me charging about on his errands for the rest of the week.'

'You get Sundays off, don't you?' she said.

'Er...yes, I think.'

'Well then, you shall come here every Sunday and continue your training. How does that sound?'

Thordric grinned and sloshed tea all down his front.

3

A DEATH AT THE COUNCIL

Thordric got to the bank barely ten minutes before it closed, and arrived too breathless to state his business. He thrust the slip of paper that the inspector had given him at the desk clerk before his legs buckled. The clerk leant over to see if he needed to ask security to drag Thordric away, but discovered he was grinning up at him. The clerk sniffed, his long nose drooping slightly, and shuffled through his papers. Finally, he pulled out a bright pink sheet, scribbling on it intently.

'Here you are...sir,' he said, dropping it over the desk to land in Thordric's lap. 'Will that be all?'

Thordric put the pink paper neatly in his jacket pocket, and then pulled himself to his feet, using the desk as leverage. 'I, er, think so,' he replied, unsure if the clerk had actually done what the inspector had wanted.

'Good day then, sir,' the clerk replied stiffly.

. . .

The inspector was in his office when Thordric arrived back at the station. He was deeply engrossed in a book detailing the plans for the Wizard Council's newest idea, spell powered carriages. He hadn't noticed Thordric enter.

'Inspector?' he said, quietly.

The inspector jumped, almost falling off his chair, and his moustache curled around to touch his nostrils again. 'Thornal!' he breathed. 'Don't you know how to knock?'

'I'm sorry, sir – I mean, Inspector. I thought you'd like to know that I completed all the tasks you gave me.' He handed the inspector the day's copy of the *Jard Town Gazette*.

'Yes, yes, get on with it,' the inspector said. 'Did the bank give you anything for me?'

'Oh yes, sir – Inspector. Erm...here.' He handed the inspector the pink sheet of paper. The inspector snatched it and unfolded it, his eyes glinting. Thordric watched them go from left to right as he read it, noticing his moustache getting more unruly with each second that passed.

The inspector screwed the paper up and tossed it in the waste paper basket, muttering something that sounded awfully like 'lack of funds'.

There was a sharp knock on the door, and a constable came in before the inspector had a chance to respond.

'Inspector, we've had an urgent call from the Wizard Council. It's High Wizard Kalljard, sir.'

'Yes? What about him?'

'He's dead, Inspector.'

'Dead? But...but...*dead*? Are you sure?' the inspector said. His moustache had gone completely straight, and it looked to Thordric as though it had turned several shades lighter than normal.

The constable lowered his voice. 'Well, he was over a thousand years old, Inspector; it was bound to happen at some point.'

'What about his eternal youth potion?'

'Perhaps it finally ran its course,' the constable shrugged.

The inspector sighed. 'I suppose you're right. I best go and see what happened and pay my official respects,' he said. He got up and put on his jacket, smoothing it down smartly. He gestured for the constable to leave, and then turned to Thordric. 'You're coming with me. If I left you here, I'd return to find the whole station reduced to rubble.'

Thordric fought to keep his expression neutral. 'As you wish, Inspector,' he said.

The inspector raised an eyebrow, not expecting Thordric to be so docile. Thordric ignored it. The inspector shrugged and led them out of the station.

The crowd was already thick when they got to the residence of the Wizard Council. It was a huge turquoise building, in the shape of a crescent moon, and had the black and silver symbol of the book and potion bottle that decorated every product they had concocted.

A group of burly constables held the crowd back from the main doors. Thordric gaped as he watched the people trying to clamour over them, simply for a glimpse inside the place. Some of them were even crying, genuine tears at the High Wizard's death, but not everyone one was there for those reasons.

Waiting for the inspector was a crumpled-looking man wearing a top hat and doing his best to bear some weight. 'Inspector!' he said, rushing up and pulling out a notepad and pen. 'What do you make of the High Wizard's sudden death?'

The inspector cursed under his breath. 'Macks! What are *you* doing here?'

'Why, Inspector, this is big news, possibly the biggest news ever in the history of *all* newspapers! Why wouldn't I be here?' Macks shrieked excitedly, his voice shrill and breathless.

The inspector's moustache broke out in curls. 'You despicable little rat,' he said. 'He only died an hour ago, and you're already seeking to profit from it.'

'Sticks and stones, Inspector,' Macks said, dancing out of the way of the inspector's fists.

The inspector growled. 'Constable!' he shouted to the one standing closest. 'Take this walking cesspit and throw him in the cells until I get back.'

'Yes, Inspector,' the constable said, and caught Macks in a grip so hard that he didn't bother to struggle.

The inspector muttered to himself, trying to smooth down his moustache. The line of constables parted momentarily to let him and Thordric through, and they found themselves in front of a set of double doors larger than most of the trees Thordric had seen. The inspector tugged on the oversized bell pull, and within moments the great doors opened to let them through.

A young wizard in full-length robes greeted them. The robes weren't black as Thordric had expected, considering it was a period of mourning. Instead, they were a brilliant, bottle green.

'Inspector Jimmson,' the wizard said, nodding his head slightly. 'We welcome you in this hour of great sadness.' He gestured for them to step inside, and the doors shut quickly behind them, leaving only the light from the blue fires hovering at the sides of the wall.

Thordric had gone unnoticed until then, but now the wizard turned to him curiously. 'And who might this be, Inspector? As you know, we have strict regulations about who we let inside our walls.'

'Oh, the boy here?' the inspector said. 'He's my errand

runner. I thought I'd bring him along so as to keep him out of trouble. Deaf and dumb, you know.'

Thordric struggled to keep his jaws shut.

'Curious. How is it that you get him to do what you want?' the wizard asked, peering at him as though he were a goldfish in a bowl.

'I write him notes, and he can lip-read to some extent.'

'Can he be trusted? We carry a lot of secrets within these walls, secrets that we would prefer not to find displayed in those dreadful newspapers.'

'Of course, of course. But I assure you, the boy could be questioned until his arms drop off before he speaks any secrets. We tested him on such matters recently, and he passed with ease,' the inspector said, without any hint of a lie touching his face. Thordric only hoped that his own face gave none of his surprise at the inspector's words away.

'Excellent,' the wizard replied, far too enthusiastically to be convincing. 'Please follow me, then.'

The wizard led them down a long corridor, past rooms where many strange smells and sounds emanated. One door had been left open, Thordric noticed, and inside he saw a bright white room where squares of different sizes and shapes shuffled themselves around on the walls, trying to connect. The inspector caught him gawking and rapped him sharply around the head with his knuckles. It hurt.

The corridor seemed to stretch on and on forever, but then the wizard made a sudden gesture with his arm. A staircase appeared in front of them, narrow, twisting, and made of hard stone. At the top was a slender gold-leafed door, embossed with the Wizard Council's black and silver emblem. The wizard paused before opening it. 'We arranged the body in his chambers for those of importance who wished to pay their respects. I must warn you, however, that in death he does not look as he did in life. Due to the magical extension of his life, his body has deteriorated far quicker that one would expect.'

The inspector bowed his head gravely, and the wizard opened the door. Inside, the room was decorated with rich velvet furnishings in deep reds and blues, and bookshelves lined the circular walls. In the middle was a grand four poster bed, and on it lay the body, covered up to the neck in silk sheets.

Thordric took in a sharp breath as he saw High Wizard Kalljard's face. The skin had become hard and leathery, curling his upper lip into a sneer and revealing several gold teeth. His hair and beard were thin and grey, hardly resembling the thick lustrous condition it had been known for. A strong musty smell came off him, although the other wizards had tried to mask it by covering the bed in flower petals.

'Great Spells!' the inspector said. 'Is this really the result of his prolonged youth?'

'It is our suspicion, yes,' the wizard said.

'How terrible. I don't suppose you have any idea what killed him?'

The wizard shifted his face, his expression becoming unreadable. 'There has been some speculation. Many, myself included, believe that he simply decided to stop drinking the potion sustaining him, although it would have taken several weeks for it to completely clear from his system.'

'So, you're suggesting suicide?' the inspector said, glancing up.

'Well, yes, I suppose you would call it that. However,' the wizard said, dropping his voice slightly. 'Others believe he was pressured into doing so. There have been a surprising number wishing to challenge his thoughts on half-wizards throughout his reign.' He shot a look at Thordric, who almost tripped over the large rug on the floor.

'You think he killed himself because of a few half-wizards? I wouldn't have thought he would lower himself to their level.'

'Quite, Inspector, quite. But it is not *I* who thinks as such. Only some of my brethren.'

Thordric shifted uneasily and went back to look at Kalljard's sunken face. He noticed that he could see the outline of Kalljard's bones under the covers, and had to shake himself slightly. He had never been good with dead bodies, even when he'd gone to visit his mother working away so peacefully at the morgue. He was about to turn away, when another smell hit his nostrils. It was tangy and metallic, like the smell of rust, but much stronger. He looked around to see where it was coming from, but noticed something odd. Above Kalljard's right ear and almost concealed by his thin hair, was a brown dot, almost like a mole; it was so perfectly round that he knew it couldn't be one. It reminded him of the paint marks he'd been practicing on the tree stump that morning, and the more he thought about it, the more convinced he was that someone had been using Kalljard's head for target practice.

With a slight sinking feeling he observed that it was a lot smaller and neater than his had been – the work of a true master. Perhaps he could practice again when he went back to Lizzie's on Sunday.

'When will the burial take place?' the inspector asked, bringing Thordric's attention back to the conversation.

'Unfortunately, it will take place no sooner than a week's time. As unexpected as this was, we haven't had an opportunity to prepare the tomb.'

'I see. Well, I humbly offer my condolences and will of course keep the papers away at all costs.'

'Thank you, Inspector. Let me show you out.'

· · ·

Once they were outside, the inspector hit Thordric sharply over the head again. 'What did you think you were doing, you great oaf?' he said to him.

'What do you mean, Inspector?' Thordric said, rubbing his stubbly head. He hardly noticed that the crowd had disappeared, leaving the constables to collect all the litter that had been left behind.

'Floating around the body, as if it were a great spectacle at the circus!' the inspector said. 'Whenever you are out of the station, you are to conduct yourself with the greatest possible dignity and poise. Regardless of your position, you are still a member of the station, and you represent everything we stand for. Behave like that again and not even your mother will be able to argue for leniency for what I'll do to you.'

Thordric quailed and tried to mutter an apology.

'Enough of that nonsense. Run back to the station and pour me a tea in the largest cup you can find, and I want a whole stack of Jaffa cakes to go with it.'

Thordric ran.

The inspector had calmed down enough after his twelfth cup of tea to ask Thordric to send for his mother. He caught the look of fear on Thordric's face and assured him he only wanted to let her know about the body. Thordric was about to leave, when he suddenly remembered something.

'Sorry, Inspector, I was supposed to tell you this earlier—'

'What is it now, Thorndred?' the inspector said wearily.

'It's your sister, Inspector. She's asked me to help her with her chores every Sunday.'

The inspector choked on his tea. 'Lizzie asked you to come back? I was hoping—' He coughed awkwardly, forgetting himself. 'I mean to say, I thought she may have chased you out with a broom, given her less than cheery disposition.'

'She said it did cross her mind, Inspector,' Thordric lied. 'But she found that I have quite a skill for fixing things.'

'Hmm. Very well then, if she wants you back, I see no reason why I should refuse to let you.'

'Thank you, sir – uh, Inspector,' Thordric said, and rushed off to the morgue.

His mother was completely shocked by the news of Kalljard's death, but was profoundly impressed when Thordric said the inspector had taken him to see the body. 'He must be starting to trust you, then,' she said cheerily. Thordric didn't have the heart to tell her otherwise.

While the inspector was entertaining his mother with the details of the whole thing, Thordric stood quietly by the wall, wishing it was Sunday already. He longed to be able to prove that half-wizards were people of value like everybody else, and he knew Lizzie's training was the key. He couldn't wait to wipe the smug expressions off the full wizards' faces when he revealed his true abilities. He could do it; he knew he could.

'Was there anything untoward about the body? Apart from its mummified state, of course,' his mother asked the inspector.

'Maggie! What a thing to ask. This is the High Wizard himself we're talking about, not the usual rough and tumble lot who find their way into your hands,' the inspector said.

Thordric's mother laughed. 'I'm sorry Jimmson, I'm afraid I get a little too carried away sometimes.'

Thordric listened, wondering if he should mention the strange rusty smell and the mark on Kalljard's forehead.

4

UNFOLDING SUSPICIONS

Thordric fought with himself all evening, pacing back and forth in his room. He began stepping so loudly that his mother had to shout up the stairs to get him to stop. He almost told her then, but his inner voice started asking, *why should he?* It was none of his business after all, and if the inspector had thought him trustworthy enough to be left alone, he wouldn't have seen anything. But he had.

Why did he care about it anyway? High Wizard Kalljard had hated half-wizards, and so Thordric had hated him. Why should he be concerned that his death was not as it appeared to be? *Because I'm decent,* he thought to himself. He was part of the local police after all, even if he was just an errand boy.

In that instant, he found he'd already made his choice and, feeling a lot less guilty, he marched downstairs to find his mother.

'Oh, Thordric,' she said, looking up from her desk. 'What were you doing up there? I thought the mountains had taken it upon themselves to crash down around us.'

'I was only thinking.'

'Thinking about what?' she said.

'About Kalljard's body,' he replied, his voice quavering a little. He coughed, forcing it to behave.

'*High Wizard* Kalljard, Thordric. Yes, I must say I've been thinking about it too. The way the inspector described it made it sound fascinating, I would love to have a look myself, from a professional point of view.'

'I think you might be able to yet,' Thordric said, shifting his weight from side to side.

'What do you mean? The official burial will be closed casket, and it's unlikely that I'll make it with all the work I've got to do.'

'That's not exactly what I meant. I-I saw something on it, while I was there with the inspector. And there was a strange smell too,' he mumbled.

'Bodies *do* tend to smell, Thordric, even if it was only an hour or so after he passed away.'

'This was different, mother. I think it was the smell of magic, strong magic,' he said earnestly.

She raised her eyebrows. She hated him mentioning magic. 'Well, he was a wizard, Thordric. If anyone were to smell of magic, I would suspect it would be him.'

'No, mother, listen to what I'm trying to tell you. There was a brown dot above his ear, and that was where the smell was coming from. The rest of him only smelt old and musty. The dot looked like it had been marked there by magic.'

She drew herself up at this, and Thordric knew he had said the wrong thing. 'How do you know it was put there by magic?' she said, her voice cold.

Thordric didn't answer.

'Thordric?' she said, her voice an octave higher. Still, he said nothing. He didn't need to, for she had already guessed.

'Thordric Manfred Smallchance! You have been trying to do magic, haven't you? Tell me why, this instant!'

He gave in and told her. 'But you could have injured yourself...or worse!' she screeched.

'I wasn't in any danger; she wouldn't have let me do it if I was.'

'She? *She?* Who is this *she?*'

'The inspector's sister,' he said, and told her all about the inspector sending him over there to help with chores.

'Lizzie? Why...she...I...' she said, flustered. 'But she's such a grand lady, I can't imagine her even considering marrying a half-wizard, let alone teaching my own son such, such...' her voice trailed off, struggling to find the words. Suddenly she got up and dashed to pick up her coat from the rack. 'I'll show her what she can teach you,' she snarled, grabbing him by his collar and marching him out of the door.

It was dark by now, and purple fires hung in the air, giving them light. Thordric, despite his mother's clamping grip, stopped to look at them. They had been yellow like normal fire the last time he had been out this late; that new rainbow magic was really catching on.

His mother didn't let him dawdle for long, increasing her grip as though she thought he might run off.

With this pace, they arrived at Lizzie's house before midnight. Despite the lateness, Lizzie answered the door fully dressed and without any hint of surprise. Thordric sighed as he saw that she'd put her hair in a tight bun again; back into schoolteacher mode.

'Why, Maggie,' she said to his mother. 'It's been such a long time, please come in.' She stepped aside so they could go through, greeting his mother's glare as if it were one of the warmest smiles in the world. 'Hello, boy. I didn't expect to see you so soon, considering all the to-do at the council.'

Thordric mumbled a greeting back, glancing at his mother to see if she was going to start shouting again, but she was too taken aback by Lizzie's welcome to speak. Lizzie led them into the kitchen, where the kettle was already boiling on the stove. 'I assume you still have milk and one sugar, Maggie?' she asked.

'I do, y—' Thordric's mother began, but Lizzie was already talking again.

'I know why you're here, Maggie. You've come to tell me how wicked I am for teaching Thordric how to control and use his magic.'

'Yes,' his mother said quietly, having lost her steam.

Lizzie handed them both tea and pulled out the remains of the cake she had made earlier. 'Have you considered, Maggie, that all this nonsense about half-wizards that the council spreads is exactly that —nonsense?' She paused, taking a sip of tea. 'Half-wizards are only half due to their parents, Maggie. It doesn't necessarily mean their magic is any weaker than a full wizard's. Your boy here probably has powers equal to those on the lower levels of the council.'

'But everyone knows that half-wizard magic ends in failure in the end. It's documented in history,' his mother said.

'Yes, the failures are indeed well documented. What is left out is how many half-wizards have actually managed to use their powers successfully.'

'What do you mean, how many? Half-wizards are rare; the ones documented were the only ones around at the time.'

'Oh, don't be so naive, Maggie! Half-wizards are every-where, but they're too afraid to try out their magic, since everyone tells them from the moment they're born that they're doomed to failure. Thordric here has tremendous potential, but if he wants to avoid making a mess of things, he has to be trained.'

Thordric's ears perked up. 'You-you think I have potential?' he said.

'Of course I do, boy. I wouldn't be bothering with you otherwise. You had so much pent-up magic that it would only have been a matter of time before you accidently caused a disaster with it.'

'But that proves the Wizard Council's theory!' his mother burst out. 'Half-wizard magic is dangerous.'

Lizzie banged down her teacup, splashing tea and cake crumbs everywhere. 'Margaret Smallchance,' she blared. 'Stop believing what the council says and use your own brain. *All* magic can be dangerous without the proper training. My poor husband spent most of his life trying to hone his powers and use them without causing harm. Full wizards don't have to do that. Their training starts when they are merely toddlers and they never have to suffer such risks as he did. Do you under-stand now? Half-wizard magic only fails because they don't get the chance to train it as full wizards do.'

She sank back in the chair, bringing out the handkerchief again to dab her eyes. Thordric's mother sat there gaping. After a moment she managed to clear her throat. 'I, um...I'd never thought of it like that. Do you really believe Thordric can be as great as a full wizard?' she said.

'Oh, Maggie, wake up,' Lizzie said, straightening. 'Thordric doesn't need to be as great as a full wizard. He can be great as a half-wizard.'

At this, two fat tears appeared in his mother's eyes, and she began weeping too. 'I'm so sorry, Thordric,' she said. 'Please have my approval of your magic lessons.'

Thordric fell off his chair. 'Y-you approve? Really?' He got up and rubbed his side. His mother inclined her head, and a huge grin spread across his face. He hugged her tightly, and Lizzie too, before dancing around the kitchen again. Somehow the copper kettle had resumed its role as his dancing partner. Then, in a moment of clarity, he let go of the kettle, ignoring the pain as it hit his foot. He needed to tell Lizzie about Kalljard!

Stuttering with excitement, he retold his story of going to see the body, and of the strange smell coming from the mark. 'The mark was like the ones you asked me to put on the tree, Lizzie, only a different colour,' he said.

'You're certain?' she asked.

'Yes, but it was more refined than mine.'

'Well, well, well,' she said, tapping her cheek with her fork. 'Maggie, I think you'd better get the inspector to release the body over to you. It seems there has been some foul play after all.' She suddenly let out a girlish squeal. 'How exciting!'

The next morning Thordric appeared in the inspector's office with his mother at his side. Ignoring the inspector's curling moustache, they explained what Thordric had seen on Kalljard's body.

'I have to examine it, Inspector. Just to be sure,' Thordric's mother said.

'I don't know about this, Maggie. How can he be certain what he saw?' he replied.

'He wouldn't lie, Inspector.' She paused. 'Please, Jimmson, do this for me. We have to know, after all.' She fluttered her delicate eyelashes at him, and he shifted uncomfortably in his chair. Thordric tried not to snigger.

'I-I'll see what I can do,' the inspector replied at last. 'No promises though, Maggie. They won't like releasing the body to us.' He got up and put on his jacket and coat, smoothing down his moustache again. 'I'd best be off over there then,' he said.

'Oh, we're coming with you, Inspector,' Thordric's mother

said. The inspector's moustache stuck out again at her words. 'I am the official pathologist after all; it would look highly suspicious if I wasn't present. And Thordric was there last time, so you may as well take him this time, too.'

'Fine,' the inspector said. 'But let me do the talking.'

'I must warn you, Inspector, that this is highly inappropriate,' the wizard who had led them around before said. 'We shall need to hear the grounds on which you base this ill-considered theory of yours!'

They were in the entrance hall of the Wizard Council. No one would let them go any further without an explanation. At least half of the members were standing around them, and Thordric could almost feel their anger.

'Calm yourselves,' the inspector said. 'We simply need to carry out a simple post-mortem to find out the true cause of death. I know it is against your usual protocol, but the circumstances were certainly unusual.'

'Nonsense! There was nothing unusual about his death,' the wizard said. 'He simply felt he had lived long enough and thought it was time for his eternal rest.'

At this another wizard stepped forwards from the crowd and put a hand on his shoulder, standing a full head higher than his friend. He looked solemnly at the inspector and sighed. 'It is strange that his reverence would not think to inform us of his decision, though. Even you cannot argue that, Rarn,' he said. 'If the inspector here believes that is adequate ground to open an investigation upon, then we must accept it.' He tuned to the inspector. 'Forgive me, Inspector. I am Wizard Vey, one of the candidates for the position of High Wizard. I'm afraid my brethren are very set in their ways. Perhaps we can have lunch together and discuss the matter further?'

'That would be delightful,' Thordric's mother said, giving a slight curtsey. The inspector caught the look she gave Wizard Vey, and his moustache bristled. He bowed stiffly, motioning to Thordric to do the same. Vey clapped his hands, dispersing the angry crowd of wizards and ignored their rude comments.

He took them down the corridor and made a sharp left to another corridor, making his shoulder-length dark hair sway to the side. Thordric had deep suspicions that the building changed with the wizard's will, for he certainly hadn't noticed a corridor leading left before.

The corridor was slightly lighter than the previous one, and the fires hanging by the walls were a pleasant pink. There were no doors to the sides to reveal what went on, simply a long steady path that sloped up gently.

Just when Thordric's feet began to ache, they came to an ornately carved door depicting a cherry tree in full blossom. Wizard Vey opened it, and Thordric blinked. The very same cherry tree was now in front of them, for real. They were in the council's garden, and he had to admit that it was even lovelier than the rumours described.

Although the cherry tree was the main feature, situated in the very centre, other trees surrounded the area, all as delicate-looking. Thordric couldn't help gazing at them as Vey led them to a large, oval table, carved from rose quartz. He sat down and noticed a tree directly opposite him. It had a blue trunk and bright yellow leaves; the one next to it was purple and didn't have any leaves at all. Instead, the branches were covered in soft-looking fur. He soon found that the cherry tree was the only normal tree in the whole garden.

'You will forgive me for the long walk here, won't you?' Wizard Vey said, pouring Thordric's mother and the inspector a glass of sparkling white juice, made from a fruit that had the power to induce instant giggling in anyone under the age of twenty. Thordric frowned as he was served only water.

'Why, of course,' Thordric's mother said, beaming. The inspector had to quickly cover his moustache with his hands to stop her from seeing it curl up to his nostrils.

'We have so few guests, I thought it only right to bring you here,' Vey continued, smiling slightly so that his short beard parted down the middle. 'Still, it does seem a shame that we have to talk over such a macabre subject.'

With his moustache smoothed down again, the inspector spoke up. 'Macabre as it may be, it is of the utmost importance. I'm sure your brethren would feel much better knowing the true cause of his death.'

A young wizard with trembling hands appeared from behind one of the stranger trees, balancing four bowls on his arms. He served them quickly, and to Thordric's delight he found that the starter was one of the special rainbow soups that had recently been developed. Every time he dipped in his spoon, it changed to a different colour, though to his disappointment the flavour remained the same.

'Tell me,' Vey said. 'What exactly is it that has caused you such concern? Rarn told me yesterday that you hardly looked at the body, other than to pay your respects. He did mention that your errand boy here seemed very curious though.' He looked at Thordric with interest, and Thordric opened his mouth to speak, but remembered the inspector had said he was deaf and dumb. However, the movement hadn't been lost on Vey.

'What is it you saw, boy? Don't be afraid to speak,' he said. He seemed so much more trusting than the other wizards that Thordric had met that he didn't hesitate.

'A small dot above his ear, you say?' Vey said afterwards. 'Yes, I admit magic does sometimes leave a mark like that.

Although what someone was doing practicing magic on High Wizard Kalljard is anyone's guess.'

The inspector broke in. 'We strongly believe it had something to do with his death. It does sound a lot like a target mark,' he said.

Vey's eyes widened. 'Surely you're not suggesting...'

'I'm afraid so,' the inspector said. 'My pathologist and I strongly believe that High Wizard Kalljard was murdered.'

5

ODOUR OF MAGIC

W izard Vey sat there blinking. His soup lay cold in the bowl, untouched, as he tried to absorb what the inspector had just told him. Thordric hadn't thought about how much of a shock it would cause everyone to say that Kalljard had been murdered. Who would be brave enough to do it, and why? High Wizard Kalljard had been *the* most powerful wizard in history.

'What...what needs to be done?' Vey said after a moment.

'Well, as we mentioned earlier to...er...Rarn, I believe you said? Yes, well as we mentioned to him, you'll need to sign the body over to our pathologist here so she can make an official report,' the inspector said.

Vey sighed, 'Very well. It will take a few hours though, as I need approval from all the council before I can do it.'

'Do you think you can get them all to understand?' the inspector asked, raising an eyebrow.

'I have no doubt. I'm sure that as soon as I explain the situation, they'll be only too anxious to discover who the killer is,' Vey said with conviction.

'You do realise, of course, that if he truly was killed by magic, then it puts the whole Council under suspicion?' said the inspector.

'Yes, Inspector, the thought had crossed my mind,' Vey replied. 'This will be a blow to everyone if it's true; our whole way of life will change if people start to doubt us.'

The inspector rose, extending a hand to help Thordric's mother, while subtly kicking Thordric in the shin to stand up. 'We will be discreet, Wizard Vey. If it is someone on the council, then the papers shall never find out.'

'Thank you, Inspector. And thank you, young man, for speaking up. Had you not, we would all have been deceived.' Vey held out his hand to Thordric, who shook it respectfully, despite the sharp pang that ran through him as their hands touched. It was probably his magic clashing with Vey's. At least, he hoped so.

Back at the station the inspector sent out two constables to find Macks, the reporter he'd clashed with the day before. Having had no grounds to keep him in, he'd been forced to let him go, but with all the new developments, the inspector wanted Macks where he could keep an eye on him.

Thordric was set to his normal duties again, and was in the act of making the inspector a fresh batch of tea when the constables came back with Macks struggling in their arms. 'I'm telling you, you have no right to do this! What is it you think you can charge me with, eh?' Thordric heard him say. The inspector must have heard too, for he emerged from his office with a grin so large it obscured his moustache.

'Ah, Macks, so good to see you,' he said, bouncing on his heels. 'I'm afraid that your cold-hearted display for the High Wizard's death has earned you some more time in the cells.'

'What a load of nonsense! You can't keep me here based on that! That's why you had to release me yesterday,' Macks said, still struggling.

'I beg to differ; I've had word that you've been snooping around trying to get a glimpse of the body so you can write about it in that foul paper of yours. Such disrespect for the head of the Wizard Council leaves me no choice but to lock you up until after the official burial. After all, there are laws dealing with *public menace*,' the inspector smirked.

Macks made a rude gesture at the inspector, which earned him a hard kick in the back of the knee, sending him crashing to the floor. The inspector chuckled and gestured for the constables to drag Macks down into the cells. Thordric watched them go, forgetting the tea he'd been brewing. The inspector saw him.

'Thornby, stop gawping,' he said.

Thordric looked down, and noticed that the tea was now almost three times as strong as the inspector liked it. He groaned and poured it away to start again. When it was finally ready, he took it into the inspector's office with a generous plate of Jaffa cakes and laid it all on the desk. The inspector gave it a single look of acknowledgement and waved Thordric away to the far wall, where he always stood when he had no tasks.

He watched the inspector dip one of the Jaffa cakes into his tea, cursing as someone knocked on the door and it sank to the bottom of his cup.

'Come,' the inspector said, fishing into the cup with his fingers. A constable entered and waited patiently while the inspector retrieved the soggy Jaffa cake and ate it.

'What is it, constable?' the inspector asked.

'We've had word from Wizard Vey, Inspector. He has managed to attain the approval of all the council members and is signing the release form as we speak.

'Excellent! Thorsted, go and tell your mother that she should be receiving the body shortly.'

Thordric didn't hesitate. He left the office, hurrying past the constables' desks, and went out into the bright afternoon sun. He shivered. Despite the brightness, the cool thrust of winter had begun to set in.

He ran to the morgue, arriving with a curious mix of sweat and numb limbs. His mother was sitting in her office, busy writing a report.

'Hello, Thordric,' she said, looking up and setting down her pen. 'I can only assume that you've come to tell me I'll be getting the body soon.' Thordric nodded, and they heard a tap at the main door. '*Very* soon, apparently,' she said. 'Let them in while I set up my equipment.'

He opened the door to find four members of the Wizard Council personally delivering it. They had wrapped it in a deep purple velvet sheet, covering it completely, and had placed it on a rolled glass stretcher. He wondered how no one had seen them bring it here. 'Please, try not to damage his reverence's body too much,' one of them said, casting a suspicious eye at Thordric.

'Don't worry, gentlemen,' his mother said, gliding across the room towards them. 'I will be as gentle as I can.'

They put the body down onto the work slab and huddled out of the building. Thordric shut the door after them and turned to see his mother delicately removing the velvet sheet. It came free easily, and she gasped as the face was revealed. They had clothed the body in a simple white robe, which she removed too. 'I knew he'd deteriorated, but I didn't expect him to look like *this!*' she said, staring.

Thordric thought he heard a slight catch to her voice, but when she spoke again there was no trace of it. He supposed it was a shock. 'Is this what he looked like when you saw him yesterday?' she continued.

Thordric, from his position floating by the door, went to have a closer look. 'Yes,' he said, somewhat surprised that it hadn't deteriorated further.

'If the council come out with any anti-ageing potions, remind me not to take them,' she murmured. She placed a hand on the body, nodding to herself. 'As I suspected, his skin has hardened.' She made a note of it on her clipboard. 'Where did you say that mark was?'

Thordric showed her, and she made another note. He could still smell the strong metallic odour of before. It must have been a very powerful spell.

'Are you certain it was made by magic? It looks like an ordinary mole to me,' she said.

'I'm certain. The smell is still there, too.'

'Smell? Are you sure?' she asked.

'Yes,' he said, adamantly.

'Okay, I'll make a note of it. I wish I could compare the mark to something.'

Thordric caught her hint, and slightly nervous that she would disapprove, focused his powers and landed a red mark on one of the anatomical figures dotted around the room. He fetched it over, and his mother held it next to the mark on the body.

'Well, aside from the colour difference, it does look awfully close. But yours is slightly rougher than that one,' she said.

'It doesn't smell as much, either,' he said, frowning.

She ignored him and made to rub his mark off. It wouldn't go. 'Now that's interesting. If I can't remove his one either, then I could be certain of it for sure.'

She tried it, at first using water, but when that failed, she used some of the chemicals she had, including some acids. Nothing worked. The mark remained untouched.

'I think you're right, Thordric. It really was put there by magic.' She thought for a moment. 'Go back to the inspector and tell him what we've discovered so far. I'll carry on with the post-mortem and see what else I can find.'

The inspector almost purred when he heard the news, and was so pleased that he gave Thordric the rest of the day off. Thordric, of course, hurried straight off to Lizzie's so she could continue teaching him.

He found her waiting for him on the doorstep. 'I had a feeling you'd be coming,' she said, smiling.

She led him into the kitchen again, where she promptly found him some more things to mend. When he tried to use his magic on the first one, an old pot so black inside that it looked like she'd used it to store coal in, he found he couldn't concentrate.

Lizzie watched him struggle. He got more and more flustered by the minute, and finally gave up and threw his hands in the air. With a yelp, he found that he'd propelled himself to the ceiling, and was now floating up there, hitting his head as he bobbed up and down.

'It seems like you've had an exciting day,' she said. 'I'll fetch out some cake and you can tell me all about it.' She disappeared into the pantry, leaving him still bouncing into the ceiling. He tried to push against it in the hopes that it would send him sailing towards the floor, but it just made him bob about more violently.

She appeared again and set the cake down on the table, and then brought out a rope from under her arm. She threw it up to him and said to tie it around his foot. He did so, bending over so that he could reach, and found that he was now upside down. He got dizzy as the blood rushed to his head. Lizzie tugged on the rope, arm over arm, and he flipped back up as she slowly lowered him to the floor. When he was at ground level, she tied the rope tightly to the table in case he floated off again.

'There,' she said, sitting down. 'That wasn't so difficult, was it?'

After he had eaten a rather large amount of cake, Thordric told her everything that had happened since he and his mother had left her house the previous night. Her eyes widened when he told her about being taken to the Wizard Council's private garden for lunch, and a smile touched her lips as he revealed what his mother had discovered so far.

'Well, that is quite the story,' she said when he had finished. 'So, you were able to make a mark without any hesitation? That's good. It shows your training is starting to sink in.' She untied the rope from his foot, and to his amazement he found he was able to stay seated in the chair.

'I'm not floating,' he said.

'You've calmed down now, that's why. My husband learnt that magic is always harder to control when you let your emotions get in the way.' She placed the blackened pot back in front of him. 'Try again.'

He did. It worked straight away; the pot was gleaming as though he'd been scrubbing it for hours.

'Good,' Lizzie said. 'Carry on with the rest. I have some work to do. Find me when you've finished.' She got up and left the room, leaving him there.

He gritted his teeth as he looked at the huge pile and went about fixing them all one by one. It began to get easier with each one he fixed, and within half an hour he had finished. Standing up with a huge grin on his face, he went off to find Lizzie.

She was in one of the rooms upstairs, and had covered her dress with a large white overall. Tins of bright paint lay around her feet, and she had a paintbrush in one hand. Half of one wall had been painted a bright green.

'You've finished already?' she asked.

'Every last one,' he said, pleased with himself.

'You're learning fast then.' She looked around the room, her eyes alight. 'Think you'll be any good at painting?'

'I did help mother redecorate a few years ago,' he replied.

'Good.' She picked up another paintbrush and gave it to him. 'I need you to paint the back wall in this orange,' she said, undoing one of the paint tins. He dipped his paintbrush in, about to brush it along the wall.

'Oh no,' she said. 'You have to direct the brush with your powers, not your arm.'

'I-I can do that?'

'Of course you can,' she said. 'Think of your mind as an extra hand, and feel the weight of the brush in it.'

He tried, and the brush flopped about and fell on the floor, marking the floorboards with a large orange splotch. 'Are you sure this is possible?' he asked.

'Yes, yes. My husband used to do it all the time. Try not to paint the floor too much, because you'll be the one clearing it up.' She turned away, continuing to paint her wall green.

He looked at his brush, still weakly flopping about on the floor, and groaned inwardly. With a mighty push, he willed it to float up to shoulder height. He watched it hover there, trying to direct it over to the wall. Instead, it came towards him and hit him in the face with such force that he staggered back and put his foot in the paint tin. Lizzie turned around to see his face and half of his leg covered in orange paint. She laughed so hard that her hand went weak and she dropped her own brush.

Thordric scowled and used the same technique he'd been

working with to clean the pots on the paint that he was covered in. He felt an odd sensation of something very hard and thin scraping across his face and leg, and saw the paint being forced off him into a giant floating ball. Trying not to lose his focus this time, he grabbed the paint tin and held it under the ball. He released the ball and it fell neatly into the tin with a wet splat. He then turned to Lizzie, who was still watching him, and made a grabbing motion with his arm, lifting her paintbrush up and floating it back into her hand from where he stood.

'I told you it was possible,' she said. 'You've just got to be determined.' After that, he managed to keep his brush floating in the air and had painted most of the wall when they heard a knocking from downstairs.

'Who on earth could that be?' Lizzie said. 'I'm not expecting anyone at this hour.' She put down her brush and took off her overall. 'Wait here,' she said.

6

UNOFFICIAL DETECTIVE

Thordric put down the paintbrush and put the lid back on the tins of paint. Quickly checking his uniform for stray flecks, he headed downstairs to see why Lizzie had called him down. When he reached the front door, he saw a constable standing there speaking to her. He looked at Thordric gravely and beckoned to him.

'The constable here says my brother needs you back at the station,' Lizzie said before the constable could open his mouth.

'I'd better be going then,' Thordric said. 'I resealed all the paint tins, ma'am, and the wall should be dry soon. Please don't hesitate to ask if you need any more chores doing.' Lizzie raised her eyebrow slightly but knew he was right to be formal in front of the constable; questions would certainly be asked otherwise.

The constable tipped his helmet to her, and Thordric copied, miming with his bare head. As they turned their backs on her, she closed the door, but he could feel her eyes lingering on them. He wondered if the constable felt her watching too, but if he did, he certainly showed no sign of it. He didn't speak to Thordric for the whole journey back to the station, and

Thordric's body tingled with the need to know why he'd been summoned.

He knocked on the inspector's office door, entering after the muffled reply from within. His mother was in there waiting, and the inspector immediately stood up and offered him a Jaffa cake. Thordric felt his jaw drop. He took it as though he'd been offered a nugget of pure gold. The inspector watched him eat it before clearing his throat.

'There have been some more developments that I believe you should be made aware of. Maggie, would you care to tell him?'

Thordric's mother smiled. 'After you left, Thordric, I carried out a full post-mortem on the body. At first, I found nothing out of the ordinary apart from the state of his skin, but then I looked at his stomach contents. It was full of potion.'

'Which means,' the inspector carried on, 'that the theory the other wizards have about him not taking it is nonsense.'

'Yes, Inspector, I remember them speaking about it,' Thordric said. 'But if he was still taking the potion, then what was it that caused his skin to go like that?'

'That,' the inspector said, rocking back and forth on his heels, 'is exactly what *you* are going to find out.'

'Me? But how?'

'Maggie here is convinced that you have honed whatever powers you have so that you can control them.'

'Um—'

'Don't worry, Thordric, he's not going to punish you,' his mother said.

'She's right, Thormble, at this moment I'm not interested in how or why. Frankly, we've never had a case like this, and indeed we don't believe anyone in the world has. We're out of our league, and, though it almost shames me to admit it, we need someone of your type to help us figure out exactly what was done.'

Thordric blinked several times. They wanted *him* to help with the investigation? To use his magic? It was unheard of.

'May I sit down for a moment, Inspector? My legs seem to have gone weak,' he said, collapsing into a chair before the inspector could reply.

The inspector coughed. 'So, er, as I was saying. You are to act as detective, unofficially, of course, we can't risk this getting out to the papers.'

'I thought we had Macks in the cells?' Thordric said.

'We do.' The inspector picked up a Jaffa cake, speaking again with his mouth full. 'But there are plenty of other reporters around here that are almost as ruthless as he is, and they would pounce on it like a lion on its prey.'

Thordric thought for a moment. 'But I don't know anything about detecting. Where would I even start?'

'Nonsense, you started already by finding that mark on High Wizard Kalljard's head. All you have to do is find out what type of magic caused it and whether it had any influence over his death. It should be easy if you *truly* have talent.' As the inspector said this, the corners of his mouth lifted into a smirk. He was testing him.

'What if I need to get back in to look around Kalljard's chambers? They won't let me in if they find out what I am, and there could be tons of clues in there. Magic leaves traces, you know,' Thordric said.

'If that is the case, then I shall accompany you and say that it is I who is looking for clues. You are my runner, after all, and seeing as you have been there twice now with me, I don't believe they'll turn you away,' the inspector said.

'It will be fine, Thordric,' his mother said, getting up. 'Oh, I've put the potion I found in High Wizard Kalljard's stomach in a jar. I'll need you to find the rest of it so we can confirm that it truly is his everlasting youth potion.'

'I'm sure I can do that...' he said, hoping his uncertainty wouldn't show in his voice.

The inspector got up too. 'Well then,' the inspector said, screwing up his face in deep effort. 'Thor*dric*, you had best be getting some rest. Off you go, and be back here early, ready to work.' The inspector really was serious about this: he'd gotten his name right.

As he walked home through the dark streets, lit with bright green fires this time, he felt so light that he could skip, but behaviour like that would hardly get him taken seriously. Neither would his current appearance, come to that.

That night, standing in front of his mirror, he had an idea. If he could force dents out of a kettle, perhaps he could force some hair to grow on his head. He stood there, gazing at his reflection, noticing how much stubble had grown back on his scalp, and also the fine hairs covering his upper lip. He willed it all to grow.

Nothing happened at first, but then it started lengthening inch by inch. It got to the length he wanted, covering the tops of his ears, with a moustache neatly spread across the top of his lip. He pulled back his powers so that it would stop. It didn't.

He willed and willed to make it stop, but that only made it grow faster. It launched past his shoulders and then his waist, without any sign that it would halt. He panicked.

Scrambling about, he looked for scissors or a knife to cut it with. The noise made his mother call up the stairs, but when it didn't stop, she appeared in the doorway.

By this time, Thordric was barely visible under the great mass of hair and moustache, and at first, she screamed, thinking he was some sort of beast. Then she caught sight of one of his hands. 'Thordric! What in Spell's name have you done?'

'I can't make it stop,' came the muffled reply.

'You must be able to,' she said. 'Maybe do whatever you did in the first place but reverse it?'

'It doesn't work!' Thordric said. His feet and hands were all tangled up in it and he could hardly move. 'Stop, stop, STOP!' He followed it with a long trail of swear words that turned his mother pale. To both their surprise, it worked.

Thordric let out a sigh and fell to the ground, exhausted. Quickly, his mother found the scissors and cut a hole around his face so he could breathe properly.

'Before I cut the rest, I believe an explanation is in order,' she said.

'I just wanted some hair,' he moaned. 'I wanted to look respectful, like a detective should.'

'Oh, Thordric! It's not appearances that make you respectful, it's how you act. If you want people to take you seriously, then you have to act seriously.'

'I know...but I think I should have some hair at least.'

She thought for a moment. 'Alright, as long as you keep it neat. I won't have you walking around with a mess like you used to have. And no moustache.'

'But—'

'*No* moustache.'

'Okay, mother...' he said glumly. She took up the scissors again and started cutting off the great lengths of hair, leaving the amount he wanted. She cut the substantial amount of moustache, and then produced a razor so he could shave off the rest himself. He went to the bathroom and came back a few minutes later with cuts all along his lip. His mother had no sympathy.

'Next time you have a brilliant idea concerning magic, talk it over with Lizzie first. Perhaps then it won't turn into such a catastrophe.'

.   .   .

The next morning Thordric found himself back at the morgue with his mother, examining Kalljard's stomach contents. The potion hadn't been fully digested yet, and so remained the bright pink that would be in the rest of the bottle when he found it. He took a small vial of the potion from his mother and put it in his pocket, grimacing.

'What do you think about the mark?' she asked him. 'Is it likely that it killed him?'

Thordric thought for a moment. 'I don't think so. When I made that mark to show you, all I was thinking was to put a dot on something. It's not really any different to putting a dot on someone with a pen or a paintbrush.'

'So, would you say it's possible it was a target mark?'

'Well, er, I suppose so. I need to speak to Lizzie to find out if it's possible to kill anyone just by marking them though. I don't know enough yet to be sure.'

'Make sure you find the potion first. If it turns out that it isn't what he usually took, then you might not have to look into the magic at all.'

He left the morgue and went back to the station to find the inspector, who was waiting for him at the front desk, twiddling his moustache. His eyes shot to Thordric's new hair and he opened his mouth to say something, but thought better of it. Instead, he coughed and said what he had been waiting to say.

'I have announced to the station that this investigation is officially taking place, and the Wizard Council has been informed of it too. Now would be an opportune moment to go there and explain about the developments we know of.'

'Yes, Inspector.'

'Keep a low profile and don't make it too obvious that you're the one looking for something.' The inspector picked up his coat, and together they made their way over to the Wizard Council's building.

The wizard known as Rarn let them in again, although he was much less courteous now he was aware he was under suspicion. He led them back along the corridor, and Thordric noticed that the doors along it were now wide open so they could see nothing sinister was going on. Clearly the council didn't like being suspects.

Instead of leading them up the staircase to the High Wizard's room, he took them to the only door that was shut, on the left. Rarn knocked politely and waited. The door opened after a moment by itself, and Rarn led them inside. Wizard Vey was sitting at a large oak desk piled high with books. 'Hello, Inspector. Thordric,' he said, looking up. 'Rarn, you may leave now. Thank you.'

Rarn left the room and Vey gestured for them to sit down. 'You are here on official business, I presume?' he said.

'I am afraid so, Wizard Vey,' the inspector replied. 'I need to have a look around the High Wizard's room. There may be something still in there that will tell us who his attacker was.'

'I understand, Inspector. I will ask, though, that you try not to move anything if possible. There are documents in there that have to be kept in strict order.'

'Of course, we – I mean to say, *I* – shan't disturb anything unnecessarily.'

'Very well, then. I'll show you up.' He led them out of the door and up the stairs into Kalljard's room. At once, Thordric was hit with an overwhelming feel of powerful magic. He wondered how he hadn't noticed before, but then it was only natural for him to start recognising magic now that he was using it more often.

'Take as long as you need,' Vey said, before leaving and shutting the door behind him. They heard his footsteps going back down the stairs, and once they were sure he was back in his office, they began to have a look around.

'Notice anything yet, Thornaby?' the inspector said, looking around the bed. Thordric sighed. He had known it wouldn't last.

'Yes, Inspector,' he said, and told him about the magic.

'Huh. Can you tell if it was done before or after he was killed?' the inspector said, now digging around in one of the drawers.

Thordric had no idea. 'I'm not sure, Inspector. I'll need to have a talk with my teacher and find out if there's a way to determine it.'

The inspector went and sat on the bed, nodding approvingly as he tested the mattress. 'This teacher of yours, is he a – the same as you?'

'No, *she* isn't. Her husband was though, which is why she knows so much about it.'

The inspector raised his eyebrows. 'My sister was married to a – one of your type. I never got on with him myself, but she thought the world of him despite his, uh, failings. Used to tell her...' He looked at Thordric, and his moustache sprang out like a fur cone. 'She's teaching you, isn't she!'

'Yes, Inspector,' Thordric admitted. 'You shouldn't be angry with her. She's teaching me the magic I'll need to solve this case.' He was looking at Kalljard's desk as he spoke. It was full of loose papers, each specifying the plans for new spells and potions. He read them all briefly, but couldn't see anything suspicious about them other than the fact that they hadn't been signed yet. Opening the drawers, he felt around inside, but there was no sign of any bottles at all. Where would Kalljard have hidden it?

He scanned the room, ignoring the inspector burbling on about his sister. *There!* His eyes locked onto the bed post, just above the inspector's head. There was a faint outline on it, as though there was a hidden compartment. The inspector watched him curiously as he went over to it and put his hand on the wood. Finding the edges, he tried to prise it open with his fingers. It wouldn't budge.

7

INTENSIVE TRAINING

Thordric attempted to force the compartment, digging his nails into the slots aggressively. Still it didn't open, and he looked around for something more substantial to use as a lever. He tried some of the pens on the desk, and then his house keys, but nothing quite fit. He was about to give up when the inspector pulled out his moustache comb. It was thin and made of metal, with teeth sturdy enough not to bend. Perfect! Thordric snatched it up, almost jarring the inspector's finger up his own nose, and prized it into the small gap. He tugged at it, and with a small pop, a cube of wood shot out and landed at his feet.

In the space where it had been was a glass bottle inlaid with silver, half full of pink liquid. Thordric pulled out the vial of Kalljard's stomach contents and held it up against the bottle. The colour of the potion was an exact match.

'So, he really had still been taking it,' the inspector said. He raised an eyebrow. 'Strange that he didn't use magic to hide the bottle, though.'

'The building is full of magic, Inspector. I'm sure most of

the members here could break any magical seal easily, and would probably look for one.'

'So, he did what they would have least expected and hid it the normal way? A smart man,' the inspector mused. 'Shame his killer didn't do the same thing. None of this messing about trying to figure out what magic was used and when.'

Thordric said nothing. He put the bottle and the vial into his pocket, and pushed the wooden cube back in place, leaving no trace that they'd found anything. He surveyed the room again, still feeling the magic that'd been used there.

'I'm sorry, Inspector, but there's nothing else I can do here at the moment. I have to go back and talk with Lizzie. There are still lots of things I need to learn before I can figure this out.'

The inspector grunted. 'Very well. At least we've found *something* here.' He got up, muttering something under his breath that sounded to Thordric suspiciously like 'Not a complete waste...'

They left the room, and found that Wizard Rarn was waiting for them at the bottom of the stairs. He eyed them up, the corners of his mouth dipping, but said nothing. He led them back along the corridor, and Thordric saw some of the wizards that had been working in the rooms come to see them go. He could sense their dislike towards himself and the inspector for questioning their ways. He felt no sympathy for them.

As soon as they were out of the building, he felt himself relax. The breeze cooled his face and drew away the intensity of the magic that had stifled him so much. It struck him how ridiculous the Wizard Council truly was. All they did was make spells and potions that didn't have any meaningful use. None of them used their magic to heal anyone or help rebuild something after a fire or an earthquake. All the magic they sold to normal people was useless.

. . .

He found his mother in the morgue, busy making notes on her latest occupant. He gulped as he peered over her shoulder to read what she'd written, turning several shades greener. He shook himself to recover slightly, and presented her with the bottle and vial full of potion.

'Ah, wonderful. I'll need to filter them before I can be certain, though,' she said, taking them and pouring some of each into test tubes. She labelled them carefully and then went into the store cupboard to bring out the rest of her chemistry apparatus. 'I'm fine with this myself. You can go to the inspector and find out what he needs you to do next.'

Thordric left to the sound of her heels clacking on the tiled floor, and headed back to the station. As usual, he went into the inspector's office, planning to ask if he might go to Lizzie's and train with her, but when he opened the door, he found her sitting in the chair opposite the inspector. She looked at him, a deep smile on her face, but the inspector had no such smile. Thordric turned to him and saw his moustache was curling up to his nose again.

'Hello, boy,' Lizzie said. Her hair bun was larger today and not nearly so tight, and she'd put on a dress and bodice in a deep burgundy. Thordric was suspicious that she'd known the inspector would find out what she was doing today, and had come to fight her case...and won.

'Thormble,' the inspector said in a strained voice, nodding for him to sit down. 'I believe you've become quite acquainted with my sister, Elizabeth—'

'Lizzie,' she said. 'Don't be so tiresome, Jimmson.'

The inspector glared. '—with my sister, *Lizzie,* then. Since she says she's happy teaching you, and I don't see any other options to solve this case quickly, I'm giving you a week's leave to learn what you need to figure this all out.'

'A week's leave?' Thordric was so stunned that his voice

came out as an excited whine. He jumped up, preparing to dance around the room again, but caught the state of the inspector's moustache and sat down quickly.

'You should run along and tell your mother, boy,' Lizzie said. 'And pack a suitcase too.'

'A suitcase? Are we going somewhere?'

'Well, I can't teach you what you need to know here in the town, the people are far too nosey. My dear husband owned a house a skip away from Watchem Woods. It'll be perfect for you to train there.'

'Wh-when do we leave?' he said.

'Today, as soon as you're ready,' she said calmly.

Thordric fainted.

Thordric woke up to find the inspector about to slap him sharply on the face, and quickly sat up to stop him. The inspector let out a small sigh.

Thordric saw Lizzie still sitting there in the chair, and his mother was there too. She seemed to have had time to go home and pack him a large suitcase full of clothes, which now sat by her chair.

'Thordric? How are you feeling?' she said to him, putting her hand on his forehead to feel his temperature just as she had done when he was a small boy. He felt his face grow hot under the eyes of Lizzie and the inspector, and brushed her hand away quickly.

'I'm fine...really...' He wobbled to his feet and sat in a chair. 'How long...?'

'Only an hour or so,' Lizzie chimed in. 'I helped your mother pack for you. We thought it would be easier to leave you here until we were done, in case you got more excited and used your magic clumsily.'

Thordric scowled. 'Looks like I'm all ready then. Shall we go?'

'One moment, Thordric,' his mother said. 'I thought you and the inspector would like to know that my tests on the potions have given me conclusive evidence that they are indeed one and the same. There are a few more tests I have to carry out, of course, but I'm fairly certain they'll give me the same result.'

'Hmmm,' the inspector said, twiddling his moustache. 'That Rarn fellow seemed so convinced that Kalljard had stopped taking it. Perhaps he was trying to convince us of it, too.'

'I'm not sure, Inspector,' Thordric said. 'I don't think he would have the initiative to do something like that, even if he was involved.'

'Well, you could be right, Thornsby, but don't forget he is a *full* wizard. I'm sure he shows his intelligence and talent within his work. He wouldn't be in the council otherwise...'

'Jimmson, you know as well as I do that the council accepts *all* full wizards, regardless of their abilities. I'm betting our boy here has more talent in one nostril than this Wizard Rarn does,' Lizzie said.

The inspector's moustache twitched. 'As I was saying, Thornaby, the point is to not let your feelings get in the way. You have to look carefully at every suspect, and pick up on the slightest detail that might prove their guilt.'

'Yes, Inspector,' Thordric said.

'A very interesting pep talk, I must say,' Lizzie said, standing up and brushing off her dress. 'I'm afraid we really must be off now, though. You'll have to find someone else to serve your tea and Jaffa cakes.'

. . .

The carriage jolted violently as Thordric and Lizzie went on their way to the house near Watchem Woods. He'd never been in a carriage before, and found it strongly disagreed with him. His face was pale, and sweat was dripping down his forehead. His body ached so much it felt like he had a fever.

'Nonsense,' Lizzie said when he told her. 'Just a little travel sickness, that's all. You *could* use your magic to lessen it, you know. Perhaps I'll tell you how so you know for the journey back.'

He mumbled a weak reply, and turned his head to look out the window. They went past posh, three-storey houses, and the smell of a bakery whizzed up his nose. They were in the rich part of town, only a few streets from the Wizard Council. How could they have spent so long in the carriage and *still* be in town?'

Suddenly, the carriage jolted over a stretch of cobbled stone, and he promptly passed out again.

Thordric's eyes snapped open as a loud hooting sound assaulted his ears.

The carriage had stopped moving, and he found that Lizzie had gone. He opened the door to get out, but missed the step and fell forwards into a puddle. He spat out the water in disgust, and was about to get up when he saw the house in front of him.

The walls were made of grey stone, and it was two storeys high. What made Thordric stare the most, though, was simply how long it was. It was the length of twenty carriages, and that was only the part he could see! The rest of it disappeared into the depths of the forest.

'Ah, young master, you're awake,' the driver said, spotting Thordric on the floor. He wore a thick leather jacket that showed a woollen lining, and leather gloves. Even so, he rubbed his hands together against the cold that Thordric now felt. 'Please tell the lady I'll be heading off now. I'll be back in one week.'

He got back up onto the carriage, and flicked the reins of the great horses that pulled it. They trotted away with much enthusiasm. Thordric watched them disappear into the encroaching darkness, before hurrying towards the thick wooden door of the house. He pulled it open and staggered across the threshold, the warmth of a fire striking his limbs.

It was bright inside, for hanging on the walls were yellow globes letting out light. He had never seen anything like them.

Footsteps sounded down the hall and Lizzie appeared, now in a much simpler dress than she had been wearing earlier. 'There you are! I was about to come and get you. There's a hot meal waiting for you if you want it. This way.' She turned, but noticed he wasn't following. 'What is it?' she said. Thordric pointed towards the globes, his mouth agape. She smiled. 'An invention of my husband's. He was very fussy about always lighting candles and sconces on the wall and thought it would burn the wallpaper. So, he developed these to use instead. They work using a special potion that gives off light for nearly eight hours when shaken, and as soon as it dims, all you have to do is shake them again and it'll light up.'

'That...that's genius!'

'I know. Food is waiting. Come along,' she said, and walked back down the corridor. Thordric followed her, suddenly aware of his stomach growling loudly.

The kitchen was a long walk from the entrance, and Lizzie led him down corridors that twisted and turned so much he wasn't sure which part of the house they were in. When at last they got there, Thordric found a large wooden table laden with plates and cutlery, and the most delicious smell coming from the great black stove that took up half of one wall. He sat down at the table and watched as Lizzie pulled out a large stack of roast potatoes and an entire chicken, and more vegetables and sauces than he'd ever seen. His mother certainly didn't cook like this; she never had the time to. Usually he did the cooking, which was limited to stew, pasta, and rice dishes.

'Where did all this food come from?' he asked, piling up his plate with as much as he could fit on it.

'I ordered it to be sent here yesterday, and it arrived this morning. I told the delivery boy to use the skeleton key I keep under the hedgehog statue outside. We've got enough for the whole week. Even if you do eat this much every day,' she added, eyeing up his full plate.

'That must have cost an awful lot of money,' he said, wolfing down a potato.

'It did,' she smiled. 'Fortunately, my dear brother is paying for it, so you don't have to worry.'

Thordric choked on his peas. 'The inspector actually offered to pay?'

'Well, no, but I persuaded him. You're a valuable member of the station, even if he's too stupid to admit it to himself. He knows full well that they can't solve this case without your help, therefore your training, as I pointed out to him, is of the utmost importance.'

Thordric finished his meal, uncomfortably full, and Lizzie showed him to his room. It was, as with everything else in the house, enormous. The bed was a double, and he found his suitcase on it waiting to be unpacked. Two large oak wardrobes stood on either side of the room, and to his amazement he found a door that led to his own private bathroom. The bathtub was white porcelain and had a tap fitted on it, quite unlike the battered tin bath he had at home.

'Can I have a bath?' he said, running his hand over the smooth surface.

'Of course. In fact,' she said, sniffing. 'I highly recommend it. The tap only lets out cold water though, so you'll have to heat it up yourself. And I don't mean by using the stove.'

8

FIREWOOD

Lizzie left the room, leaving Thordric to run his bath. The water was icy. He wouldn't be able to bathe in it; he'd freeze after only a few seconds. She certainly knew how to stop him from taking short cuts.

Rubbing his eyes to try and get his brain working again, he decided to let the bath fill before trying to heat the water. While it was running, he unpacked his suitcase.

His face went scarlet when he saw his underclothes on the top layer, for he remembered that Lizzie had helped his mother pack it for him. He hastily threw them into one of the drawers inside the closest wardrobe. Next were his shirts and tunics, followed by his trousers and socks and, going red again, his thermal vest and long johns. At the bottom was a bottle of Wizard Council enhanced cough medicine, a toothbrush, and the pair of scissors his mother had used to cut his hair.

By this time, the bath was almost full to the brim. He turned off the tap and knelt by it, contemplating the best way to heat it up. So far, he'd learnt that most things done by magic had to be visualised as though he were doing them by hand, like painting, and fixing the kettle. He was confident that if he thought about the water being on a hot stove, it would do the trick.

It did – too well.

He dipped his finger in and brought it out again, wincing as a blister started to form. Getting a metal coat hanger from one of the wardrobes, he carefully unhooked the plug to let some out, and then replaced it again. He turned on the tap, letting in the icy water, and waited for it to cool the rest down to a bearable temperature. It didn't take long.

He stripped off, eager to soak in the now warm water, but the door sprang open and Lizzie came in with a pile of fluffy pink towels. 'Sorry,' she said, putting them on the bed without noticing his nakedness. 'I couldn't find the white ones.'

Thordric hastily covered his private parts with his hands and tried to sidle behind the bathroom door so that she couldn't see. Unfortunately, she looked up before he got there, and started to chuckle. His face began to feel as scolding as the bath water had been.

'Don't be so silly, boy! There's nothing to hide about. I did have a son of my own once, you know.' She threw a towel at him to reduce his embarrassment. He quickly wrapped it around himself, trying to keep some amount of dignity against the pinkness.

'You never told me that,' he mumbled. 'Besides, I'm almost a man.'

She chuckled. '*Almost*, but not quite.' She turned to leave.

'Wait,' he said. 'You said used to. What happened to him?'

She sighed and sat down on the bed. 'He ran away. Right after my husband died. He was a year or so older than yourself at the time, and I spent ten years searching for him. Eventually my heart couldn't take anymore and I gave up looking.' She sniffed, making Thordric feel rotten for asking, but still he felt compelled to know more.

'Was he a half-wizard too?' he said.

She rubbed her eyes and straightened up. 'I thought he would be, but he never showed any signs of it. My husband tried to teach him a few things despite that, but he couldn't pick it up, and he didn't have any interest in it either. Anyway, that's enough of my talk. You'd better get in the bath before the water cools again,' she said, and left the room.

She knocked on his door early the next morning, saying that breakfast was ready. Thordric opened his eyes and looked to the window. It was still dark outside. He groaned.

Dragging himself out of bed, he pulled on some fresh underclothes and trousers, and fished around for one of his warmer tunics. He put on his boots and clumped down the stairs, trying to remember which corridor to take to get to the kitchen. He decided to go left, but found that the light globes were only lit partway and so turned back to go the other way. After several more wrong turns, he found himself in the kitchen where Lizzie had laid out a hot bowl of porridge for him. He ate it hungrily, wondering where she'd gone. His answer came a moment later when she breezed in through the door, alarmingly carrying an axe.

'Don't be long finishing that, I've got your first task set up in the garden.' She put the axe on the table beside him. 'You'll need that,' she said.

He stared at it, his spoon hovering in the air near his mouth. 'You want me to chop firewood?'

'Yes, it gets cold in here if I don't keep the fire burning.'

'But you want me to do it by magic?' he asked.

'Of course. I didn't bring you all this way to have you doing things manually.' She shook her head, busying herself with the kettle. He thought for a moment, finishing his porridge.

'I don't see how that's going to help me recognise what magic was used.'

'Then you're not using your brain,' she retorted. 'Have you finished?'

He handed her his bowl, picking up the axe to head outside. 'Don't sulk, boy,' she added, watching him slouch out of the room. 'And I want it chopped nice and neatly.'

As soon as he opened the door, the wind hit him full in the face, knocking him backwards. He steadied himself, and stomped off to where the woodpile was.

Staring at it, with tears in his eyes both from the wind and how high the pile was, he clenched his jaws and put the first piece on the block. He set the axe down on the floor, and tried to lift it using the same technique he'd used for the paintbrush. It rose slowly into the air, making him shake slightly as he adjusted to its weight. Miming the movement with his hands, he chopped at the wood. The axe followed the movement but missed and bounced off, narrowly missing his foot. He jumped back, swallowing, and tried again.

The axe went into the air easier this time, but when he swung it, it only clipped off a small bit of wood. His swing was too weak, he had to put more power into it, and precision too, else Lizzie would make him do it all again.

Preparing himself, he tried a third time. This time, he managed to make it chop into the top of the wood, but it stuck hard and wouldn't come out. He tugged at it with his magic, and then with his hands. It wouldn't budge.

Gripping the handle tightly, he planted his foot on the wood and pulled and pushed in all directions. Sweat began to drip down his back despite the cold, and with one mighty tug, the handle popped out of the axe head. Thordric lost his balance and found his backside planted in the ground, the axe head glinting in the sun as though cackling gleefully.

Grinding his teeth together to stop himself from cursing, he got up and forced the handle back into the metal head. He put more force on the wood with his foot, and slightly less on the handle, and pulled. The axe came out cleanly in one piece, and flew into the air to land behind him.

'I'll get you this time,' he muttered, looking at the block as though its very presence offended him. He lifted the axe back up by magic, his resolve making it sail into the air, and swung it down with all the force he was capable of. It split the wood right down the middle, even on both sides. 'Hah!' he said, picking up the axe again and swinging it around like a sword.

'I presume you are aware of how dangerous that is,' Lizzie said, appearing by his side. Thordric jumped a few feet into the air.

'I-uh, I just...' he mumbled.

'Yes, I was watching,' she said. 'Now, cut the rest of the pile like that and I'll consider serving you lunch.' She disappeared back inside, closing the door with a bang.

Several hours later, with his muscles aching and blisters inexplicably appearing on his hands, he trudged into the kitchen, where the smell of Lizzie's cooking made his stomach growl. She glanced at him and tutted, before bringing over a bowl of warm water to soak his hands in.

'I don't understand,' he said, gratefully immersing his hands. The warmth spread through his fingers and the throbbing of his blisters eased dramatically. 'I hardly even touched the axe once I got the hang of it. How can I have blisters and ache so much?'

'My husband called it *Phantom Exhaustion*,' she replied, setting up the table. 'It comes from convincing your body that you're using it when you're not. It'll wear off once you get more used to this kind of magic.'

'I sure hope it does. I'll be in agony for the rest of my life if it happens every time.'

They had stew and freshly baked rolls for lunch, which Thordric ate eagerly. Once he had finished, Lizzie asked him to bring in the wood he'd chopped, using magic again. This he found easy, and managed the whole pile in only three runs. After he'd done that, she called him into the kitchen. He almost went back out again when he saw the stack of pots she'd produced from him, but she caught him by the arm and plonked him into the chair in front of them. It was only then that he noticed that they were all gleaming and without so much as a scratch on them. He looked at her suspiciously, wondering what she wanted him to do.

'Now you've woken up your mind, it's time for you to try something new.' She gestured to the pots. 'As you can see, these are all in perfect condition. What I want you to do is mess them all up. I want dents and scratches, handles bent out of place, and scorch marks.'

He stared at her, both his eyebrows raised so high that they met with his hair. 'You want me to damage them? Are you sure?'

'I'm certain. But,' she said, staring at him sternly, 'I only want them to *look* that way.'

'But...err, what? How would I do that?'

'You have to make an illusion, boy,' she said, rolling her eyes.

'Make an illusion? Why do I need to learn to do that?'

She rapped him hard on the knuckles with her rolling pin, ignoring his wince. 'You should know by now not to ask that. Fill your head with magic, not questions. I'll be along the corridor if you need me.' She left him alone once again.

He was completely lost this time. Where did he start with making an illusion? He pulled one of the smaller pots towards him, trying to imagine its shiny surface all tarnished and battered. He supposed it was possible, for she wouldn't have asked him otherwise, but his mind stayed blank.

How would he do it without magic? That was where to start, he knew, but he wasn't sure how he'd even do that. He could use paint. Yet that would change the pots' surface for real, and he was sure that wasn't what she wanted. He could cover them with something though, if he wanted to disguise them.

Maybe, if the illusion he made was a sort of blanket, he could just drape it across them? He thought about trying, but knew that if he wanted it to work properly, he'd have to do it to each one individually.

He picked the small pot up and closed his eyes, thinking of draping a white sheet over it. He opened them again. There *was* something covering the pot, but it was so transparent it was almost invisible. He sighed and it disappeared completely.

Lizzie sailed in at that moment, catching a glimpse of the transparent sheet before it vanished. Thordric saw her and hung his head. 'I can't do this,' he said.

'There's no such thing as can't, especially with someone of your abilities. You got further that I thought you would, you've only been at it for an hour.'

'But I've hardly done anything.'

'That's not what it looks like to me. You seem to have worked out how to do it already,' she said, putting some of the logs he'd chopped into the stove.

'Well...yes...' he said. 'It didn't work though.'

'I didn't expect it would on your first try. This is a very different type of magic to what you've been doing so far. It's very advanced, and it will take time.' She poured him a cup of strong tea and brought out a plate of cookies from one of the cupboards. 'Here, take a rest from that today, there are plenty of other things I have to teach you. You can try it again tomorrow.'

He sipped his tea, taking note of what she'd said. So, he was on advanced magic? He could certainly see why it was advanced, it had made him sweat more than the log chopping, and he'd been working on it less than half the time.

'How good are you with identifying plants?' she asked him after a while.

'Well, I know when we've got weeds in the garden. I've never really had to think about it.'

'In that case, this will come in handy for what I've got for you next.' She produced a small book from her apron pocket and handed it to him. He flicked through it, noticing it was all neatly written by hand. It was a list of all the wild plants in the area, starting with the most common, complete with sketches and details on recognising them.

'My husband compiled it when he started investigating the properties of certain herbs, and found that a number of the plants that grow in Watchem Woods also have interesting properties.'

'Herbs are what potions are usually made with, aren't they?' he asked, browsing through it again.

'Precisely, although you won't be making any today. All I want you to do is go out and try to identify as many as you can, using that book.'

He looked at her, and a wide grin spread across his face.

9

WATCHED BY WATCHEMS

Lizzie handed him a heavy velvet cloak. He wrapped it around his shoulders, and realised that it was the type that had sleeves. He put his hands through and did up the clasp that was level with his middle and peered into the mirror. He looked like one of the Wizard Council, except that the symbol on his chest was of a half moon, not the book and potion bottle.

'This was your husband's, wasn't it?' he asked her. He couldn't help running his hands down the smooth, soft fabric.

'Yes,' she said. 'I made it for him one winter so he could go and gather his herbs without freezing. I'm sure he would have liked you to wear it to do the same. It's yours now.'

'Thank you, Lizzie.' He pulled up the hood and opened the door, the wind catching in his face again. Picking up his lamp, and clutching the book tightly, he made his way into the woods.

At first, he followed the length of the house, finding that it actually only extended a little way in. He found a door on the end wall, but then he saw that the hinges were caked with rust. It might open if he tried ramming it. He shrugged, and then noticed there was a strange looking plant right by it. He flicked through his book, trying to find it. It was on the first page, with a note next to the picture saying, 'V. Common'. Well, it might be common here, but Thordric had never seen it before. It had a long thin stem of darkish green, and instead of flowers it grew giant purple ball-like things. He supposed they were a fruit of some kind, but he checked the notes to see.

Big Man's Nose (Vicus Ruberus): Grows in vast numbers throughout all woodland areas, bulbs grow in place of fruit. Collect stem and bulb. Properties: reduces temperature, mild sedative.

So, they were bulbs, then. He picked one, despite what Lizzie had said about only identifying, and put it into his pocket. He moved on through the trees, and soon found what her husband meant when he'd said it was common. The woods were full of it. In every direction clumps of it had grown almost to the height that he was.

He trudged past them, going straight forwards into the heart of the woods, and almost trod on a small clump of delicate yellow flowers. They grew barely an inch off the ground, and as he knelt to have a closer look, he caught the loveliest fragrance he had ever smelt, similar to coconuts and vanilla, with a hint of rose petals. He opened his book, and found it about a third of the way in.

Winsome Sunbeam (Oppulus Nuvendor): Grows in small clumps, difficult to spot. Only present in some areas. Collect flower only. Properties: induces hallucinations of varying intensity dependant on dosage. Dangerous if used frequently.

. . .

He decided he wouldn't be picking that one too soon, unless he wanted to use it on someone he didn't like. He smiled, imagining what would happen to the inspector if he slipped a little into his tea. No, the inspector wasn't bad enough for that.

Walking further into the woods, he identified ten more plants he'd never seen before. Some cured headaches and fevers, others helped to reduce swelling and heal bones quicker, and one even prevented hair loss. He was taken aback by how many uses they had, for he saw frequent notes written beside each one, telling him how to combine them to create different effects.

He searched eagerly for more, but the deeper he went, the more it felt like he was being watched. He looked around, lifting his lamp high in the growing darkness, but he couldn't see anything. Shrugging, he carried on, but then a branch snapped behind him, making him jump. He turned but again saw nothing. 'I was sure...' he began, but then one of the bushes started to quiver. It slowly transformed, growing thinner and more twig like, with sharp spiny fingers and a beard of fuzzy leaves. It only reached up to his kneecaps.

Thordric stayed still, the hand holding the lamp shaking slightly and casting the creature in quivering shadow. It crept up to him, standing on two legs, and began sniffing at his cloak. He winced as it poked him with its sharp fingers, and it let out a strange warbling noise that he thought sounded suspiciously like laughter. Seemingly satisfied, it warbled at him again and then scampered off into the trees. Thordric swallowed.

He suddenly remembered the book in his hand, and flicked through it desperately to see if the creature was in there. It was, at the very back on the last page.

. . .

*Watchem Watchem (Nexus Traubus): A creature that camou-
flages itself as a bush. Gentle but usually very curious. If they
find you friendly, then they may permit you to take a leaf from
their beards. Properties: cures fatal illnesses, opens the senses.*

Now at least he knew why the woods had such a peculiar
name. He closed the book, realising how stiff his fingers had
gotten from the cold. It was fully dark now, and Lizzie would
probably be expecting him back. He wrapped his cloak tighter
about him and tramped back to the house, resisting the tempta-
tion to pick the various leaves and flowers of the plants he had
identified.

The house was blissfully warm inside, and he went straight
to the kitchen to further warm his hands by the stove. Lizzie
was busying herself cutting up potatoes and carrots when he
entered.

She raised her eyebrows at him, noticing the slight bulge in
his pocket where he'd put the bulb of *Big Man's Nose*. 'I
thought I told you only to look?' she said.

He grinned at her. 'I couldn't help it. There are so many
plants in there that I've never even heard of, and I even came
across a Watchem Watchem.'

'You saw one? Patrick – that is, my husband – was the only
person I've ever known to see them up close. I've only caught
glimpses.'

'It came right up to me – almost made my heart stop when I
saw it transform,' he said, sitting down at the table.

'Yes, I remember Patrick telling me the same thing. He
went to visit them often when we lived here; he grew quite
friendly with them.'

. . .

Breakfast the next morning was even earlier than the last, but this time Thordric descended the stairs eagerly. When he got to the kitchen, he found that the table had been moved to the side of the room, and a large cauldron, decorated with a mosaic pattern, was in the centre. It was Thordric's turn to raise his eyebrows. Lizzie handed him his bowl of porridge with a smile on her face.

'I think you're ready to begin learning about potions now. A nice simple one for today, I think. You can carry on your illusion practice while it's brewing,' she said.

He spooned in a mouthful of porridge quickly, burning his tongue. He'd forgotten all about the illusion spell. 'What, er, potion will it be?' he asked, fanning his tongue with his hand.

She dug in her apron and produced another book from it, handing it to him. It was handwritten like the other one, and was labelled 'Potions for useful purposes'. Thordric snorted at that, given the ridiculous potions that the Wizard Council always developed. He recalled that one of their more recent ones was designed to make ladies feet temporarily shrink slightly to fit the latest high fashion shoes better. His reaction wasn't lost on Lizzie.

'My husband wasn't overly fond of the Wizard Council, he believed they should be using their powers for greater things,' she said. 'Have a look and see which potion you feel like attempting. Only the ones marked simple, mind.'

He opened the book. Only the first ten pages covered simple potions, and there were four to choose from. The first one was to help the drinker sleep, the second cured – to his delight – travel sickness, the third was one to cure stuttering, and the fourth was to prevent contraction of the common cold. He hovered over the one for travel sickness, but then remembered how quickly he got colds in the winter and decided to make that one instead.

'Well, then,' Lizzie said when he told her his choice. 'Find out what the ingredients are and then go and gather them. I'll show you how to prepare them all when you get back.'

He finished his porridge then headed back out into the woods. He looked at the book and saw he needed to find three different plants. Two of them he had seen the previous day, but there was one he didn't recognise and it was marked as very rare. He went after the ones he knew first, taking the exact quantity stated then roamed around, scanning for the one he didn't know.

The woods looked different in the morning light, and he could see that the bushes were all different colours, ranging from deep purple to bright yellows and greens. A number of them quivered, and he suspected that most of them were Watchem Watchems. A few even let out the strange gurgling sound as he passed.

He checked in his book of plants to see what the new one looked like, but the entry showed several variations. The note by it said it was a shape-shifting plant, and only revealed its true shape in pure sunlight at midday. It wasn't anywhere near midday yet, so how was he supposed to find it? He threw his hands up in the air, suddenly aggravated, and slumped down by one of the trees, flicking through both books to pass the time.

He'd been reading for only a few minutes when he heard a rustling sound. He looked up, and found he was surrounded by Watchem Watchems. They were studying him, with their dewdrop-like eyes staring at the books in his hands. One, a dark blue colour, prodded the book of plants.

'What are you doing?' Thordric said, startling back a few inches. The creature prodded the book again, and then made to grab it. 'Hey!'

Still the creature prodded it, and the others started to join in, more insistent. He watched them, and decided to see what they wanted. He put it on the floor in front of them. The dark blue one opened it up, turning the pages until it landed on the page with the plant Thordric needed. It pointed to Thordric and then to the picture. 'What?' Thordric said. The creature made a small noise like a sigh of exasperation, took the potion book from him, and laid it on the floor, turning the page to the prevention of colds potion. It tapped the ingredients, and then the picture of the plant in the other book.

Finally, Thordric understood. 'You know it?' he asked. The creatures all nodded. 'You know where to find it?'

They nodded again, and ran off to his right, gurgling all the while. He gathered up the books and got up, stumbling on his cloak so that he was propelled head first into a tree. The Watchem Watchems gurgled even more as he righted himself, shaking his head to try and make his vision return to normal. They waited for him, but as soon as he was able to walk again, they scampered off ahead.

Fifteen minutes later they stopped around a single, unremarkable plant. He walked up to them, looking at it. 'Are you sure this is it?' he asked. The dark blue one prodded him hard in the shin, and then pointed at the plant. 'If you say so.' Thordric picked the plant and put it in the small bag that held the rest of the ingredients. The creatures purred, and before he could thank them, they all ran off.

10

POTS AND POTIONS

Lizzie made him lay out all the plants on the table, and then they opened the potion book to the right page. 'You didn't have to pick the whole plant, you know,' she said, tutting as she read the instructions.

'I didn't have a knife with me to cut off the right parts,' Thordric said.

'Hmm.' She spread the plants out into three separate piles, and read out what parts of each they needed. The first one he'd plucked was needed for its roots, and she picked one up and handed it to him. 'Here.' She gave him a knife, and then took one for herself. He went to cut his, but she smacked him hard on the knuckles.

'Not so rough, boy. Do it gently, and with precision. The roots need to be cut into inch-long pieces for it to work properly.'

He carried on, doing as she said, and she muttered approvingly as she watched. Then they moved on to the next plant, which used the leaves, ground up to a fine powder, and the final plant had to be stripped to the stem. It took a while to make

sure it was all done to the standard that the instructions specified, but once it was, all they had to do was put the right
measurements into the pot and wait several hours to let it brew
and thicken.

'There's nothing else we have to do? No words or
anything?' he asked, slightly disappointed.

'You could say some words if you like, but I doubt it'll have
any effect. Not all magic uses the power of the wizard, you
know,' she replied.

'Oh,' he said.

She moved over to the cupboards, taking out the pots and
pans he had been trying to create an illusion over. 'There's
enough time for you to get a bit more practice in before lunch.
Don't worry about speed, just concentrate on your technique
and it'll come.'

Thordric looked at her doubtfully, but sat down at the table
anyway. She put the pots in front of him, and then drifted over
to the stove to finish preparing lunch. Thordric rubbed his face,
thinking about how he managed to produce the transparent
cover last time. He picked up one of the smaller pots again,
turning it around in his hand before setting it back down.

Picturing the white cloth on it, he willed it to appear.
Slowly, as if it were gently growing, a faint whiteness started to
become visible over the pot, gaining substance as it grew. Sweat
built up in beads along his temple, but he kept at it and soon
the pot really did look like it was covered in cloth. He stopped
for a moment and put his hand out. The pot still felt like metal,
and the illusion stayed. Now all he had to do was mould it to
make it appear as though the pot was old and broken.

He thought of staying with the cloth idea, and had to make
it fit the pot's shape rather than simply covering it. He pushed
the image of the cloth down inside the pot, almost as if he were
creating a lining. It wasn't easy. It resisted every slight touch he

made, and the exertion had started to make him shake again. His mouth went dry and his nostrils sore, but he was too determined to stop. With a final push, the cloth illusion gave way and clung to the inside and outside of the pot like he wanted.

With a small cheer, he scrambled out of the chair to show Lizzie, but as soon as he turned, he felt the room shift about him and his legs buckled. He remembered taking one last, long breath before the blackness took him.

He woke to find he was still on the floor, but now he was sitting upright near the stove, and Lizzie had wrapped a blanket around him. He went to peel it off and stand up, but he felt a sharp rap across the top of his head. 'Don't move, boy,' Lizzie said, brandishing her rolling pin above him.

'But—'

'Do as I say, and don't argue. You overdid it with that illusion spell, and you need to lie still for a good few hours. I would have taken you to your room myself, but skinny as you are, you seem to weigh a great deal,' she said, returning to the stove and stirring one of the pots.

'I only got the shakes a bit—'

'And then you passed out. You're pushing yourself too hard, I said to take that spell slowly. If you'd been a full wizard and trained at the Wizard Council Training Facility like all the rest, then you wouldn't even know about it until you were eighteen.'

'B—What? You said they start their training when they're toddlers. It takes them that long to get up to advanced magic?' he said.

'Yes, it does. That is why no member of the Wizard Council is under thirty, because their training takes that long. You've learnt more magic in the few days you've known me than they learn in three years.'

'Surely they're as quick at learning as I am?'

'No, boy, they aren't. As I said before, you have a tremendous amount of magical talent, in fact, far more than I originally thought.'

Thordric felt his head buzz at what she'd just told him, and with a large grin on his face he fainted again.

'Boy? Boy, wake up, lunch is ready.'

Thordric opened his eyes lazily and yawned. The cauldron in the centre of the room was bubbling away musically, and the smell of Lizzie's cooking charmed him so much that he ambled up, supporting himself on the wall, and staggered over to the table. It had been cleaned since they'd chopped up the plants, and the odd bits of root and leaves had been replaced with large bowls of steaming food. In the middle was a plate of freshly baked bread, and his mouth hung open as the smell from it reached him.

'Eat well, boy,' Lizzie said, sitting down at the far end of the table. 'Food will replenish you.'

Thordric didn't hesitate. After filling his plate, he started eating great chunks of meat and stacks of vegetables and potatoes. He felt better after each mouthful, and by the time he was finished, he thought he was ready to take on the illusion spell again. Lizzie's answer was to throw a particularly large apple at his head.

'I don't care if you think you feel well enough to run to the moon. You've had enough of that spell today. You can try it again tomorrow, but today you have to finish your potion,' she said.

'I thought it was done?' he said, pointedly nodding to the bubbling cauldron.

'If you think that, then you didn't read the instructions properly. It needs to be filtered and then stirred for three hours for it to be finished.'

'Stirred for three *hours?*'

'Yes, boy. I suggest you get to it. You'll need to make a cloth for it to filter through. My husband used to weave together some of the reeds that grow at the edge of the woods. He made them into a sort of cover to put over the cauldron, so when it was tipped the potion would sieve through but leave all the bits out that aren't needed.'

'How long will that take?' he asked. She picked up another apple and aimed it at his head. He scattered.

It didn't take him long to find the reeds outside, for they lined the side of the house. He cut several armloads, wrinkling his nose at the sweet smell oozing off them, and took them inside. Lizzie led him to another room down the hall from the kitchen, where he found a small workbench and a large fire blazing away.

He sat down and stripped back the reeds so that they had no leaves left on them, and laid them out. His mother had shown him how to weave a few years ago, when she had asked him to help her mend some baskets she had, and so he set to work with ease. In and out he threaded each piece, making sure it held properly, and then added another one. It took him several hours to make a full cover that he was happy with, but when he was finished, he went back into the kitchen and showed it to Lizzie.

This time her face betrayed her surprise, and she put the cover over the cauldron to see if it would fit. It did, perfectly. 'You've done well, boy,' she said, dipping into the vast cupboards again and fetching out one of the largest pots he'd ever seen. 'Now all you have to do is hold it in place while tipping the cauldron.' She pushed the large pot beside the cauldron, and mimed tipping the potion in to see if it was close enough. Satisfied, she signalled for him to start.

He didn't ask her if she meant for him to use magic, he

knew her well enough now to know that she would likely shove an apple up his nose if he did. The best way to go about it, he decided, was to magically stick the reed cover to the top of the cauldron and then physically push it over. It seemed to be what she wanted, for she didn't object, and soon the potion had been filtered out into the pot. He let go of the cauldron and unstuck the cover, taking a peek inside. Now he understood why it'd been necessary. The pot was full of bits of plant. He'd assumed that once they'd put it all into the cauldron, it would turn into a sort of gloop. He hadn't thought that the potion only needed the essence, and with a chuckle he thought about how much it was like making tea.

'Now, I'll start the stirring for a moment while you tip that mess outside,' she said, and picked up a ladle.

He frowned at the cauldron, knowing that the only way to actually move it all the way to the front door would be to carry it by magic. Clapping his hands together he willed it to float into the air. After a few grumbling rolls about the floor, it worked, and he made it soar over Lizzie's head and out into the hall, strolling behind it.

After he'd come back and washed it out at her request, she told him to take over the stirring. 'By hand, if you please. We mustn't splash any,' she added, stepping aside and gesturing to the ladle. 'Two and a half hours left to go.'

To amuse himself, and take his thoughts away from his badly aching arms, Thordric decided to rearrange the kitchen with his magic. Lizzie was at the other end of the house, sorting through the laundry, so he knew he was safe.

He started with all the herbs hanging along the beams on the ceiling, and organised them by the colour of their flowers, working through the order of a rainbow from deepest blue to brightest yellow. He had a lot of trouble with one in particular, whose flowers changed colour depending on which way he looked at it, and ended up putting it at the end of the line, looking decidedly sorry for itself.

He then moved on to painting patterns onto the cupboards: moons, stars, swirls – and the back wall desperately needed a mural. Deciding what to put on it, he switched the direction in which he was stirring the potion to give his muscles some relief. He thought of the Watchem Watchems and how they had helped him, and knew that was what he should paint.

Starting with the background of the forest, he built up the layers of trees and shrubs. It was easier using paint from his mind, for he didn't have to think about choosing the right colours – what he remembered was the colour it became. It was fun. So fun that he didn't hear the footsteps behind him, or the clearing of her throat as Lizzie stood and watched. He carried on, now painting in himself lying by the tree, and the dark blue Watchem pointing at his book, with the others surrounding them. When he was finally done, he signed it at the bottom. He stepped back, taking over the stirring with his magic, and bumped into Lizzie.

'Hello, boy,' she said calmly.

He swallowed audibly. 'I was j-just...'

'Amusing yourself?' she offered. He shifted uneasily, unable to read her expression. She walked over to the painting, glancing up at the herbs and the cupboards as she passed, and ran her hand along the wall, the paint already dry. 'These are the Watchem Watchems, aren't they?'

'Yes...they helped me find one of the plants this morning,' he said, manually stirring the pot again to stop his hands twitching with nerves.

'I never realised how colourful they were. Beautiful,' she murmured. 'You've done a fine job, boy. I think I'll keep it.'

'Really?'

'Yes, my husband would have liked it too.' She looked at the clock on the wall. 'That should be well done now,' she said, nodding to the potion. 'We'll be able to drink it.'

Thordric looked down at the pot, and discovered that it did indeed look done. Where it had only been a translucent, pale green when he'd sieved it out of the cauldron, it was now a vibrant, almost luminous green. He stopped stirring gratefully, and stepped back so that she could fill two glasses full of it.

'Have you ever tried a decent potion, boy?' she asked.

'No, I haven't tasted any. Mother never let me.'

'Well then, I advise you to hold your nose and drink it as quickly as you can. Effective as my husband's potions are, they all taste disgusting. Bottoms up,' she said, clinking his glass with hers.

He did as she said, but the potion was so strong that he could still taste it. It was like drinking dirty dish water combined with stale milk and week-old socks. He almost gagged. Lizzie herself had gone a shade greener, but recovered quickly. 'I think I'll make some tea, and perhaps we should have a slice of cake each,' she said, her voice thick.

Thordric couldn't speak, so he simply nodded. His body felt peculiar, and for a moment his legs quivered. Then it was over, and he felt so well that he thought he could cartwheel about the room. 'Wow. That was certainly strong. How do we know if it works?' he asked.

'Simple. We shouldn't get any colds for at least six months, regardless of how much time we spend out in the cold or with people who are already ill.'

11

OUT OF BODY

Thordric shivered as he stood in the garden, which was large enough to drop the house in with room to spare. He stamped his feet, and they made muffled thuds against the snow that had fallen heavily the night before.

Despite it being mid-morning, he hadn't been up for long, as Lizzie had wanted him well-rested for this next task. She was a little way ahead of him, putting together what looked like a great tree trunk with odd branches. When she stepped back, however, he could make out what it really was: a wooden man, perhaps as tall as himself, complete with arms and legs.

'What's that for?' he shouted over to her, trying to make his voice penetrate through the wind. She flapped her hand dismissively at him, making some small adjustments, and then walked back to where he was. 'What's that for?' he repeated once she was within earshot.

She pulled down the thick scarf that was covering her mouth. 'A target.'

'A target? For what?' he asked. His ears had started to go numb by this time, so he drew the hood of his cloak up. The wind blew it back down. At least the potion seemed to be working; he didn't feel ill at all.

'It's for you. You'll see that I've made it look like a man.'

'Yes...?'

'I want you to make it move as a man would move,' she said. He gaped, thinking her suggestion as ridiculous as if she'd proclaimed that she had powers herself; everyone knew how absurd that was. Full wizards were always men, and that extended to half-wizards as well, though no one knew the reason for it. As far as he knew, no woman in history had ever had the power to do magic.

'I have to make it walk? You're sure this is possible?'

She looked at him, raising her eyebrow. He closed his mouth. 'I'll try it,' he said.

'Wonderful,' she said, and headed back inside.

'How am I supposed to make you move?' he asked of the wooden man. As expected, it didn't reply. He tried moving one of the arms in the same way that he'd lifted the axe. It worked, but it was too stiff a movement, and anyway, how would he be able to move all the limbs like that at once? He had to try something else.

He pulled at the figure, hoping that it would step forwards of its own accord if he did. All that happened was that it toppled over into a great pile of snow.

Thordric swore.

A moment later there was a tap on the window behind him. He turned to see Lizzie watching him through it, shaking her head. She opened the back door. 'There's no need for that kind of language, boy. Take it slowly and think through it. It'll come,' she said, and went back inside.

Resigned, he went up to the figure and dug away some of the snow that now surrounded it, his fingers feeling like they had all been bitten by a particularly savage beast. Once it was clear, he used his powers to raise it to its original position. He stepped back to look at it, taking in its roughly cut face and torso. Perhaps the trick was to imagine it really *was* a man.

He painted on a face and added some hair and a beard, and fetched a spare cloak to wrap around it. Trudging back to his place, he turned around and looked at it from a distance. It was much more convincing. He made himself believe that it was a kind visitor, gently strolling towards him in the deep snow, and willed it to happen. It didn't move.

He kicked at a rock on the ground, sending it hurtling off into a clump of trees. 'I was so sure that would work! Rotten fudge cakes!' he cursed politely, in case Lizzie was still about. 'So, what do I do with you?'

'Nothing, you've done enough,' Lizzie replied behind him. 'Come inside and work on the illusion spell some more.'

He followed her in, not wishing to stay outside with the figure any longer than he had to. If he'd have failed any more, he would have put his woodcutting skills to use on it.

As Lizzie was getting all the pots out for him to work on, he warmed himself by the stove and found that his fingers recovered almost completely. He decided to take his boots off and do the same with his toes. Relief spread through his body as they thawed. It was blissful.

'Come on then, boy. Show me what you can do with these today,' she said, pulling out a chair for him. He sat in it gratefully. Surprisingly, she sat down too. 'I thought after yesterday that I would stay and watch you in case you pushed yourself too much.'

He shrugged, and got to work on the spell. He picked up the small pot again, this time pulling his hands over it as if he were really covering it with cloth, and willed it to happen at the same time. He saw a fleeting smile on Lizzie's face as the illusion of cloth appeared over the pot, following his hand.

As with the day before, he made it fit the exact shape of the pot, noticing how easy it seemed now. Of course, this wasn't what Lizzie had specified it to look like. She wanted them looking battered and in dire need of repair, and for that he really would have to use his imagination.

He faded out the whiteness of the cloth, making it almost completely transparent, just enough colour to let him know it was still there. Then, as though he were painting, he began to decorate it with shading and pulled the cloth about to give it dents. This made him sweat again, but Lizzie said nothing so he carried on. More and more detail went on it, adding everything he could remember from all the pots he had fixed. He tried to get the effect right to work with the lighting but he began shaking again.

'Boy, you should stop now,' Lizzie said, but he didn't hear her. He knew he could do it, knew he could get it right, and worked in every bit of magic he had. His breathing became shallow and laboured, but he was almost there. A few more details...

He collapsed back in the chair, and weakly held the pot up for Lizzie to inspect. 'You've done it,' she said quietly. 'You really have done it.'

She got up, leaving the pot on the table. To Thordric's surprise, the illusion held, though he couldn't even tell if he was using magic to maintain it. Coming back a moment later she had a large tray filled with tea and cakes. He dug at them hungrily, the sugar immediately bouncing him up to full strength.

'You can have the rest of the day off, boy,' she said, handing him another slice of cake.

'Really? Thank y...' He stopped, the cake hovering by his mouth.

'Boy? What is it?'

'I've had a thought. The wooden man outside. You said I have to make him move like a man.'

'Yes,' she said, nodding.

'Well, I remember going to a puppet show once, and the puppeteer had a miniature wooden man, and he made it move as though it was real,' he said. He saw her smile. 'It got me to thinking, I could do that too.'

'Are you going to try it?' she asked.

'Yes. Yes, I think I am.' He finished his tea and then pulled on his boots and cloak, disappearing out the door.

Outside, the wooden man was where he'd left it, with the only difference being the amount of snow piled up around it. He cleared it away with the tiniest thought, marvelling at how easy everything got the more he did it.

'Right, you!' he called to the wooden man. 'You're going to move this time, and move well!'

Ropes appeared, attaching themselves to the head and limbs of the man, precisely as Thordric had seen at the puppet show. He pulled on them, making sure they were fixed on tightly, and then he tried to make it move. First one leg moved, then the other, with the arms swinging in opposition. It was working. He moved the head about, as though it was looking around, and made it walk several more steps forwards.

'I hate to disappoint you,' Lizzie said, walking up to stand next to him. 'But it doesn't walk the same way as a man. It still *looks* like a puppet.'

His stomach sank. She was right, of course. Even if he had gotten it to move, it wasn't very convincing at all. He had to find a way to make the knees bend, and there was no feeling of weight to its movements. But he was out of ideas.

'Have a think about it over the rest of the day. You're very close, boy. I don't imagine it will take you long to figure out.'

'I hope so,' he said as they both made their way inside.

. . .

His dreams were chaotic that night, jumping from place to place, with faces he felt he knew, but didn't, appearing everywhere. He saw the puppet moving towards a sea of battered pots. Then the puppet changed into the dead body of Kalljard, standing alongside him uttering incoherent words, surrounded by Watchem Watchems pointing and gurgling and dancing around him, around and around and around...

Sweat clung to him as he woke, and his muscles shook. It wasn't even time for Lizzie to rouse him, yet he found he was fully awake. Wanting to get out of his damp nightclothes, he ran a bath, absently heating the water as it came out the tap. He stripped off his clothes and got in, letting the warm water wrap around him like a blanket.

His thoughts turned to the station, and he suddenly wondered how the investigation was going in his absence. He felt slightly guilty that up until then he hadn't given it any thought at all. Had the inspector interviewed anyone yet? Wizard Rarn was under the most suspicion, he knew, and if anyone had been taken in, it would likely have been him. Still, Thordric couldn't see him being the culprit. His magic must have been weak, for only the wizards of lesser magic did any of the chores or domestic tasks, and Kalljard's murderer had to have been someone higher up, someone that Kalljard had regular contact with. Unfortunately, that was a very long list.

Thordric sighed and sank back in the bath. He only had a few days left of being here, and when he got back the case would be on his shoulders. If he failed, the inspector would not be pleased. He had to figure out how to move the wooden man convincingly. He wasn't sure what good it would do the case, but he believed Lizzie would only teach him magic that she thought was relevant. He would get it today. He would, if only he could figure out how to do it.

'Boy? Boy, your breakfast is ready,' Lizzie called.

He climbed out of the bath, splashing water everywhere, and quickly dried himself with one of the fluffy pink towels she'd left him. Flinging on some clothes, he went downstairs and along the corridors into the kitchen.

'Are you quite well, boy?' she asked, handing him a plate of fresh rolls and butter.

'I'm...fine. I had some bad dreams.' He crammed half a roll into his mouth, washing it down with the tea she placed beside him.

'Did they give you any insight?' she asked.

'What do you mean? It was all a jumbled mess. I woke up feeling like my head had been split.'

She chuckled. 'Sometimes when wizards dream, it helps them understand or realise certain things. My husband took a lot from his dreams.'

'Then he was lucky. I didn't get anything apart from a chill.'

Thordric headed outside again once they'd finished eating. There had been even more snow that night, and it was still coming down as he walked out. He blew away the pile of it covering the wooden man, and started thinking of new ways to make it work. He had been close with the puppet idea, she'd said. What if it had been the ropes that made it wrong? There *were* other ways to make puppets move, he knew. Like glove puppets, where it looks as though the puppeteer puts their hand up the character's backside. He didn't fancy doing that, even with a magical hand.

He kicked at the snow, idly making patterns, and walked

towards it to examine it again. He laughed as he saw that the cloak he'd put on it had frozen solid during the night, along with its hair and beard, which were full of icicles. He put out a hand to thaw them away, but as soon as he touched the figure, he felt a curious tugging sensation. He drew his hand back, wondering if it was something else, but the tugging stopped. Lightly touching it again, he felt another tug. It was as though it wanted him to be drawn into it.

An idea struck him so hard that it knocked all the other sensible ideas clean out of his head. Was it even possible? He imagined Lizzie standing next to him, preparing to take a crack at his knuckles with her rolling pin for asking silly questions. There was only one way of finding out whether it was possible or not, and that was to try it.

He pushed his hand against the wood, using his powers with it. He felt his mind sink into the grain, as softly as through butter, and suddenly he saw things from a different perspective. The wooden man had no real eyes, and apparently there was no way for him to look out from it if they weren't there. Instead, he seemed to be hovering slightly above it, and could see his body still touching the wooden man's head. He tried moving, but his body stayed still. The wooden man, however, did not.

It flapped its arms about, and then moved its legs, all in time with his thoughts. Now he saw what Lizzie had meant. He had been close, but he'd been thinking about it from the wrong perspective. He'd tried to use tools to help move it, when what he'd really needed was to move it from inside.

With his grin invisible on the wooden man's face, he made it lift his body up and walk it over to the back door of the house. There, he urged it to swing the door open and walk inside. It was odd, seeing it all from this angle, but it made him think about everything in a different way.

Directing it to the kitchen, where he knew Lizzie would be, he swung the door open and marched in. As usual, she didn't turn around right away, but spoke to him anyway. He snuck the wooden man up behind her as quietly as he could, still holding his body.

'Did you have any luck, boy?' she said. 'I couldn't hear you cursing, so I assume you—' She turned around and let out a shriek. He laughed so hard that he made the wooden man judder.

12

A SAD PAST

'Boy, don't you scare me like that again!' Lizzie said, taking refuge in a chair. 'I'm not as young as I used to be.'

Thordric tried to say sorry, but he was still in the wooden man's body and no sound came out. He slowly pulled back his mind and poured it into his own body. The sensation was very strange, going from coarse wood to warm flesh. The wooden man fell with a thud on the floor, and Thordric stood up in his real body again. He felt frozen, and had to do an athletic style warm up to work out all the cricks that had developed in his neck and back.

'You've done very well, boy. It took my Patrick nearly three weeks to figure it out, and even then, he almost had a panic attack trying to switch back again.'

Thordric grinned. 'So, what else do I have to learn?' he said, joining her as he sat down in one of the chairs.

'There are many things for you to learn, but for the investigation I believe this is everything you should need to know.'

'But none of it seems relevant. I know you say it is, but I can't see it.'

'Once you get back to town, it should all start to make sense. Remember, by learning this magic, you not only learn how to do it, but also to recognise when someone else has done it.'

He watched as she absently wiped off a mark on the table. He hesitated, 'Lizzie?'

'What is it, boy?'

'Do you honestly think I can solve this?'

'Yes, boy, I do. You have a keen mind, and you're very good at picking up small details. You'll find whoever did it, and you won't need to ask them how, either.' She got up and went over to the cupboards, getting out pots and pans. She caught the expression on his face and laughed. 'Don't worry, boy, you need a rest from spell work. I'm not about to make you practice anything yet, I'm only using them to start lunch.'

He exhaled slowly. 'What shall I do then?'

'Well, you have two options. Either you can start on that travel sickness potion, or you can help me in the kitchen. I would prefer you did the former, because I dislike other people hovering around while I cook.'

Thordric left the room quickly, forgetting his books and having to go back for them. Then he remembered that he hadn't put the cauldron in place, and went back again. He had to move the table against the wall, which meant disturbing Lizzie as she chopped up the vegetables. Finally set, he hurried outside and into the forest.

He walked along the wall of the house as before, remembering the door where he'd first found *Big Man's Nose*. He doubled back, deciding to find out how to get there from inside the house. He knew it was probably along a corridor he hadn't been down, and at the risk of disturbing Lizzie once more, he went to ask if she had a map he could follow.

'What door is this? The only doors that I know of on the

outside of the house are the front and back ones. I've never seen one at the end of the house,' she said, resting the ladle she had been using against her cheek. She'd forgotten how hot it was, and took it away again sharply, her mind back on the food.

'Well, it's there. Almost as big as the front door, but it's a reddish colour and has completely rusted shut.'

Lizzie turned to look at him. Her face was red from being so close to the stove and her bun had fallen out of place. 'I can't even think what rooms are down that end of the house, I haven't been there in so long...'

'*Do* you have some sort of map?' he asked.

'No, I – wait,' she said. Putting the ladle down in the pot, she went out of the room. Thordric wondered if he should keep stirring the stew she'd been making or check on the pie he could smell, but he didn't quite dare. He simply stood by the stove, watching to make sure nothing boiled over.

He stood there for at least a quarter of an hour before he heard her shout out to him from down the corridor. He went out to see where she was and found her in the room where he'd weaved the cover for the cauldron. She was busy unravelling large sheets of paper on the desk. He coughed as he inhaled some of the thick dust hanging in the air.

'Come here, boy, and unroll the rest of these for me,' she said. He walked up to the desk and picked up the nearest roll of paper. As well as the dust, he caught a strong whiff of mildew. He undid the silk tie around it and stretched it out on the table. On it, in faded ink, was a map of a forest. At first, he thought it was Watchem Woods, but then he saw a name written across the top: *Teroosa Forest*.

'I thought you were looking for a map of the house?' he asked, unravelling another one depicting a different forest.

'Not a map, the original blueprints. Patrick built this house himself, so they should be here somewhere.'

'Why are there so many forest maps?' he said, unravelling yet another.

'That's Patrick's doing. When he was writing that plant book of his, he travelled to all the woods and forests in the country. To make it easier for him to remember which plants grew where, he mapped them all out.'

'Oh,' he said, unravelling another. 'Hey, this one is different. I think this could be it – see, that looks like the front door there. And yes – there's the kitchen.' He pointed to the rooms with his finger.

'That is it! I knew it was here somewhere. Let me have a look.' She manoeuvred him out of the way and spread the map flat on the table. She traced her fingers over it, muttering under her breath. 'Is this where you think the door is?' she asked, tapping the end of the house.

'Yes, that's exactly where it is.'

'Hmm. Perhaps it was added after these plans were made. It's certainly not marked.' She handed it to him. 'Here.'

Thordric took it and went off back down the corridor. He noticed a cloud of smoke filtering out of the kitchen door, and hurried off in the other direction before Lizzie could scold him for distracting her.

The map led him along the corridor where the staircase to his bedroom was, but continued straight past it. It was black down there, much too dark for him to see without bumping in to anything. He felt along the wall for the light globes, and shook them. The sudden brightness made his eyes hurt, and he stumbled forward, blinking.

When he recovered, he looked at the map again. In his blindness, he had gone straight past the turning he'd needed, and had to go and retrace his steps. He lit more light globes, this time prepared for the brightness, and carried on, following the corridor until its end. The blueprints showed several more turnings to get to the room where the door should be, and he followed with the feeling that he was going the wrong way. There was something about the house that confused his sense of direction, not just the complex turnings everywhere.

He was about to turn back and go down the corridor that felt right, when he walked straight into a large room which had no door at all. He looked at the blueprint again. That should have been the room on the other side of the outer door, but there was a built-in wardrobe where he'd expected it to be. Looking around the rest of the room, he found that the walls were lined with book shelves, much like those in High Wizard Kalljard's chambers, except they were all empty. There was a desk in the centre, and a leather-backed chair, but nothing else. All of it was covered in inches of dust, and cobwebs billowed down around him. It was no wonder Lizzie couldn't remember this room.

As a precaution, he went into the wardrobe and knocked on the back of the wall, in case it was false. It wasn't. The wall was solid stone. He tried the same with the sides and with the other parts of the room where he could get to the wall. There was definitely no door there.

Deflated, he took the long walk back to the part of the house that he knew, and put the blueprint back in the room with all the maps. Still avoiding Lizzie, he scribbled down a quick note for her and pushed it under the kitchen door before going outside.

He intended to pick the ingredients for the travel sickness spell, but his curiosity was far too strong. With the weather freezing and the snow higher than his ankles, he walked along the house to find the red door again. It was still there, brushing aside his doubt that it might have been his imagination. He looked at it closely this time, and realised that the reddish colour was actually rust. He'd thought it was only the hinges that had been affected.

He stretched out his hand to touch it, but left it hovering an inch in front. Something was wrong. A strange tingling filled his fingertips, warming them. A strong suspicion grew in his mind, and he put his hand out fully and pressed it onto the door. It felt smooth, much smoother than it should have been. He smiled. It was an illusion.

Ignoring what Lizzie had said about resting his mind magic, he pushed at the illusion. He could feel how it'd been done. It was the same way he'd managed his illusion on the pot. All he needed to do was pull back the cloth-like part and the spell would lift. He tried, tugging hard, and it began to move. He managed to get a stronger grip, and with one last tug it came free, revealing what the door really was. Thordric inhaled. It was a safe.

The snow crunched behind him, and he turned to see Lizzie, dressed in a thick woollen cloak. 'Lunch is r—what is that?' she asked, pointing. 'I thought you said there was a door here?'

'I did,' he said. 'But it was an illusion. Whatever's in here, someone didn't want anyone to find it.'

Lizzie walked closer to the safe. It was much smaller than the door had been, and only a foot wide. 'I've never seen this before,' she whispered.

'Shall I open it?' he asked.

'I—yes, I suppose you should,' she said.

Ignoring the combination mechanism, he aimed his magic at the hinges. He unscrewed them and lifted the door off, crouching to see what was inside. A book, and a small, wooden flute. He lifted them out to show to Lizzie.

She stared at them, her face paling. She took the flute from him and rolled it around in her hands. 'This belonged to my son. I-I haven't seen it since he left.' She put it to her lips and played a few notes, the sound bright and cheery in the crispness of the air. 'It sounds just the same as when he used to play it.'

He saw her eyes watering, but she brushed the tears away impatiently. She held out her hand for the book, and he gave it to her. The cover had faded, and she squinted as she tried to work out what it said. She shook her head and opened it, reading a few lines. 'This is Patrick's diary,' she whispered, her tears flowing freely now. Thordric stood there awkwardly, unsure of what to do.

'Boy, come back inside with me,' she said, sniffing. 'Your lunch will be spoiling.'

He followed her back into the house, where they made their way to the kitchen. He found that she'd already served up his food on the table, which was still pushed to the side where he'd left it. He sat down wordlessly, waiting for her to say something. She didn't. She sat at the far end, flicking through the book with the flute remaining in her hand. Not wanting to let his food get cold, he started to eat, finding that he was suddenly ravenous. He was almost finished when she finally spoke.

'I never knew he'd even kept a diary,' she said. Thordric stopped stuffing his mouth and looked at her, wondering if she was speaking to him or merely saying her thoughts aloud. 'Not one about magic, at least.'

'Is that what he wrote about in there then...his magic?' he said.

She looked at him, as though remembering he was there. 'Yes...I believe so. I haven't read much, but it seems to be about the spells he tried to do, and his methods for making them work.' She flicked to the back of the book. 'What disturbs me is this last entry he wrote. He talks about Kalljard, saying he needs to be stopped. It was written the day before Patrick died.'

Thordric shifted uncomfortably in his seat. 'You think he wanted Kalljard dead?'

'Dead? No, not that. But I think he wanted to try and break up the council. He wanted to prove – like you do – what half-wizards are capable of, and to try and convince them that they have a right to be part of the council, too.'

Thordric creased his brow. 'How did you say he died again?'

'He used a spell on himself, or so the pathologist said. It went terribly wrong.'

'Do you know what spell?' he said, his stomach curdling.

'I have no idea. I was too upset at the time to think about it, and my brother didn't let me see the body until it was fully prepared for the funeral.' She reread the last page again, sighed and closed the book.

Thordric stretched his memory back to when Lizzie had first told him about her husband. 'He had an argument with one of the council members the day he wrote that, didn't he?' he said.

'Yes.'

'It seems a bit odd that he died the next day, don't you think?' He looked at her seriously, and saw his meaning pass through her eyes.

She stood up and took his empty plate over to the sink, bringing him a slice of cake and a mug of warm tea. 'It is *very* odd, boy. Particularly in light of the magic he was capable of. Who do I accuse, though? I tried telling my brother about the argument Patrick and this wizard had had, but he said I was in shock and told me to stay indoors and rest. Shortly after that, my son ran away.' She picked up the flute again, feeling its smoothness with her fingers. 'I didn't have the strength to argue about it all after that.'

13

WINSOME SUNBEAM

The travel sickness potion was working well. They'd been in the carriage for over an hour, and Thordric hadn't felt ill at all. Now his mind was free to play back the events of the last few days, giving him time to absorb how much he had truly learnt.

Less than two weeks ago, he hadn't used his magic at all, and had known nothing about using spells or making potions. But now, thanks to Lizzie, he could. He knew how to levitate objects, paint without a brush, make inanimate objects come to life and create illusions.

In the last days at the house near Watchem Woods, he'd perfected his illusion spell and had been able to cast it over the entire stack of pots that Lizzie had laid out for him. He had pushed himself to learn everything that Lizzie taught him, and he'd enjoyed it. But now he was going home. Back to the station, back to discovering Kalljard's killer.

'What are you thinking, boy?' Lizzie asked beside him. She was clothed in her smart dress again, but Thordric had a feeling that she felt more comfortable in the country clothes she'd worn for the past week.

'I was thinking about the case. About Kalljard and the Wizard Council...and about whether they had anything to do with your husband's death.' It was true, ever since they'd found the diary it was all he could think of. To think that the council might be responsible for the death of someone who'd questioned their ways: it was disgusting. If they truly had done it, then was all the council responsible, or just Kalljard? It had been well known that Kalljard had commanded the utmost respect and reverence from everyone, so anyone challenging him would have presented a serious cause for concern.

Lizzie sighed. 'You mustn't worry about that, boy. Concentrate on finding out who was responsible for Kalljard's death. My husband was a patient man, I'm sure he would want me to be patient too. We can look into his death after all this is over.'

'If you're sure, Lizzie. But I'm nervous about dealing with the council. They'll find out that I'm a half-wizard if I need to use my magic. They won't like it.'

'No, they won't. But you have to make them accept it. You're as good as they are, and you need to assert your authority over them if you are to solve this. I believe in you, boy, but you're the one who has to make it happen,' she said. 'And ignore any snide remarks my brother makes to you. He doesn't understand magic; the thought that a half-wizard might be considered higher up than he is frightens him.'

'I...I never thought the inspector would be scared of something like that,' he replied.

She smiled. 'Our parents were very poor, and he always wanted a better life for himself than they'd had. He's a status driven man, there's no changing him.'

．　．　．

They arrived back in town after dark. The horses' hooves clattered on the cobblestones, and Thordric winced at each step they took, afraid they might wake everyone up. Lizzie asked the driver to pull up outside Thordric's house, and he got out, standing on the doorstep. She handed him his suitcase and, to his great surprise, embraced him fiercely.

'Good luck, boy.'

'Thanks, Lizzie. And thanks for everything else, too. Really,' he said.

She raised a hand goodbye, and climbed elegantly back into the carriage, tapping the roof for the driver to move on. Thordric waved until it had disappeared along the road, and then hurried inside, acutely aware of the chill air and the icicles that hung from the doorway.

The house was silent inside. His mother was either out or had already gone to sleep. It didn't matter which, for all he wanted to do was climb into bed and not be disturbed until morning.

He woke suddenly. It was still dark, and at first, he thought he had only been asleep a few minutes, but then he heard the dawn chorus of the birds and sat up to look at his clock. It was six o'clock, and he had to be at the station by seven-thirty. Blinking away his tiredness, he got up and put on his uniform, splashing unpleasantly cold water onto his face.

There was a knock on his door. It was his mother, dressed for work as usual in her high-heeled shoes. So much had happened that he felt as though he hadn't seen her for months.

'Thordric! I can't tell you how much I've missed you,' she said, embracing him even more tightly than Lizzie had done. 'Did you learn a lot? Enough to solve the case?'

She embraced him again, not giving him time to answer.

'Inspector Jimmson hasn't been able to make any headway at all. He's interviewed some of the wizards, but all he could get out of them was how much they respected High Wizard Kalljard.'

'Don't worry, mother, I'll be able to find out who did it,' he said, hardly able to breathe from the tightness of her grip. 'Please, let me go. I'll be late!'

She released her grip. 'Yes, of course. I was about to leave myself. We can go together.'

They left the house five minutes later, making it to the station in good time. Since it was so cold, both of them had wrapped themselves up to their ears in woollen jackets. Thordric sighed, wishing they were as warm as his cloak had been. Lizzie had let him bring it back with him, but it would cause too much trouble if he started wearing it, and he could ill afford that at the moment.

His mother left for the morgue as soon as they got there, leaving him to go to the inspector's office alone. The constables stared at him as he entered, but he said nothing. He knocked on the inspector's door and entered once he had permission.

'My, my, it's you, Thornable,' the inspector said, twiddling his moustache. 'My sister teach you well?'

'Yes, Inspector,' Thordric replied.

'Good, good...so, where do we go from here? Everything still stands as it did last week – oh, except for the burial that is.'

'Burial? They did it already? But what if we need the body?'

'Calm down, boy. They buried a likeness, not the real body. Of course, the people believed it was, so that information is strictly confidential.'

'The Wizard Council actually allowed that?' Thordric asked.

'No, they didn't. Fortunately for us, Kalljard's body was in such a state that none of them suspected that the body we gave them back was a fake.' The inspector chortled to himself, picking up a Jaffa cake from the plate beside him.

Thordric found it hard to speak. They had switched the body, right under the council's noses?

'Inspector?' he said, after a moment. 'Will they still let us in to Kalljard's chambers?'

'They will if I make them. It might not be any good though, Vey is High Wizard now. Elected him yesterday. He might have moved into the room already.'

'I think we should go back there anyway, Inspector. I'm sure there's something I've overlooked.'

'If you say so, Thodred. You're the one with the...er...gifts.' He smiled maliciously as he said it, and Thordric remembered what Lizzie had said. He suddenly felt an overwhelming pang of pity for the inspector. It must have shown on his face, for the inspector's moustache curled, and he ordered him to wait outside the station until it was time for them to go to the Wizard Council.

For half an hour, in the bitter cold, Thordric waited. The snow was up to his ankles, and it had started to hail. The inspector came out and looked at him with a cheery expression on his face, and it was all Thordric could do not to levitate him up onto the station's roof.

They kept a brisk pace on the way to the council, and although Thordric's fingers and toes went numb, the rest of him felt quite warm. When they arrived, the inspector, ignoring the bell pull, rapped smartly on the giant doors with his stick. A moment or so later, they swung open and Wizard Rarn stood there, his surprise all too clear on his face.

'I-Inspector, how good to see you,' he lied. 'May I inquire as to your intentions?'

'I need to look around the High Wizard's chambers again,' the inspector replied briskly.

'But surely, Inspector, you know that they now belong to High Wizard Vey?' Rarn said, almost hissing.

'Nevertheless, I need to look.'

Rarn straightened, his eyes cold. 'Very well. I'll take you to the High Wizard and he can decide whether or not to allow you to do so.'

They followed him down the long corridor, Thordric noting absently that the fires hanging by the walls were now bright red. It gave the building a warmer feel, despite Rarn's coldness. He noticed that the doors alongside the corridor were open still, but no one rushed out to look at them as they went past.

Instead of taking them straight up to the High Wizard's room, Rarn stopped outside Vey's old room. He knocked, and the door swung open. High Wizard Vey came out, looking terribly tired and not wizardly at all. His long hair fell about his face in clumps and his short beard was sticking out in all directions. 'Let them up, Rarn,' he said, without even letting Rarn speak.

'But your reverence—'

'*Do it*, Rarn. They have an investigation to complete.' He turned to them. 'I'm sorry for my appearance, gentlemen, I've been awake all night completing the paper work declaring I accept the terms of my office. They read almost as tiresome as a dictionary.' Thordric grinned. There was something about Vey that was so much more likable than the other Council members.

Rarn bowed stiffly and took them up the staircase leading to the High Wizard's chambers. He let them in and then disappeared back down it. Thordric snorted involuntarily. The room hadn't been changed at all, and the smell of magic coming from it was as strong as the last time he'd been there. Only now he knew what it was. Somewhere in the room was an illusion.

He walked around, trying to feel where it was coming from, and noticed the plant on the desk. It had been there before, but of course Thordric hadn't recognised it then. It was *Winsome Sunbeam*. Digging around in his pockets he pulled out the plant book Lizzie had given him and flicked through it, finding the page it was on. There. He looked at the properties and blinked. *Produces hallucinations, extreme use can be fatal.*

He pointed it out to the inspector, whose eyebrows and moustache both shot up at the same time. 'So, this weed is dangerous, then?' he said.

'I would say so, Inspector.'

'Wait a moment. Maggie – that is, your mother – only found potion in his stomach, and that matched his secret stash. There was nothing to indicate he'd eaten this.'

'Did she find out what ingredients were used in it?' Thordric asked.

The inspector's moustache bushed out. 'Of course she did! She wouldn't forget to do something as important as that, not my Maggie!'

Thordric raised his eyebrows, and the inspector clamped his mouth shut hastily. 'Did she tell you what the ingredients were?' Thordric pressed.

'I-uh, well, I think she said something about chalk, ivy root and blackthorn leaves. There was something that she couldn't identify, but she said it was some type of mineral.'

'So apart from that, it was all stuff he could find in town?' Thordric mused. 'Then why would he have kept this here, I wonder?' He twiddled some of the leaves around his fingers. He had to find out where that illusion was. 'Inspector, have a look around the room and see if you can find anything odd.'

'What am I looking for?' the inspector said, affronted at being asked to do something so menial.

'I'm not sure,' Thordric said, rubbing his head and realising how much his hair at grown. Wryly, he noticed that he had some stubble growing on his chin, too.

'Well, that's a help, boy,' the inspector grumbled. He set off to do it anyway, occasionally stealing glances at what Thordric was up to.

Thordric looked over the rest of the desk again, pulling everything out and feeling it to see if it was really what it looked like. He had just found a drawer full of what appeared to be fan letters when the inspector called over to him.

'Thornsby, come over here.'

Thordric scrambled over to where the inspector was standing by a large wardrobe. The smell of magic coming off it was so strong it made him cough. 'This thing looks like it's made of wood,' the inspector said. 'But when I touched it, it didn't *feel* like wood.'

'Are you sure?' Thordric asked. The inspector's moustache began to quiver; *obviously* the inspector was sure. Thordric put his hand on the wardrobe. It felt like smooth glass, not something wood should feel like at all.

The illusion on it wasn't very strong. In fact, it had been done so carelessly that he wondered how it had stayed on so long. With a simple flick of his magic, the illusion lifted free. They found themselves staring into a long, wide mirror.

The inspector's mouth fell open, and his moustache had curled up to his nose again. 'Wh-what just happened, Thorndred?'

'It was an illusion, Inspector,' Thordric said, breathing more easily. 'All I did was lift it.'

'An illusion, you say? Why would someone want to hide a mirror?'

Thordric frowned. The inspector had a point. 'I'm not sure, Inspector.' He sniffed, and his brow creased even more. There was something else still hidden in the room. Now the mirror had been revealed, he could feel it was coming from the desk. Going back over to it, he looked for something – anything – he might have missed. There was nothing.

But it had to be coming from something.

He stared at the scattered papers littered on it, and froze. He picked up one of the sheets, looking at it closely. It was one of the new spells that Kalljard hadn't signed, only there was something wrong with it. All the writing was slightly blurred, as though he were looking though a pair of spectacles that belonged to someone else. This was it.

He tried to feel where the illusion began, but it was so faint he couldn't get a good grip. He put it down, taking a few deep breaths like Lizzie had instructed him to do when he got too excited, and tried again. This time he got hold of it, yet unlike the mirror, it had been done with extreme precision. He tugged at it, but it held fast.

He tried again, but was interrupted by a knock at the door.

The inspector walked over and answered it. High Wizard Vey stood there. 'I'm terribly sorry, Inspector,' he said. 'But it seems that I have to transfer all my belongings here today. I'll have all of late High Wizard Kalljard's belongings transferred to the store room where you can access them whenever you need, but I'm afraid I can no longer grant you access to this room. I do apologise, I understand how inconvenient this must be.'

Thordric slipped the paper into his pocket.

14

LIFTING ILLUSIONS

The inspector and Thordric had no choice but to leave after Vey told them what was going on. As they left the room, Thordric saw the inspector nip a few leaves off the *Winsome Sunbeam* on the desk, and as soon as they were out of the building, he handed them to him.

'Thornsy, take these to your mother and see what she can tell us about them.'

Thordric did as he asked, and made his way down to the morgue. His mother was looking through a microscope when he entered and, as she looked up Thordric saw she was wearing a pair of extra strength goggles. They made her eyes look huge and he had to suppress his grin.

'What is it, Thordric? Did you find something?' she asked, standing up and pulling off the goggles. Her usually neat and styled hair got caught up with the straps and she had to wrestle with it for a moment to get it free.

Thordric held up the plant leaves and gave them to her. 'These are from a plant we found on Kalljard's desk. I didn't recognise it when we went there the first time, but I do now. It's called *Winsome Sunbeam* and it can...'

'Produce very strong hallucinations? Yes, I've come across it before. Some of the people I've performed post-mortems on took it.'

'How is it taken?' Thordric asked.

'Usually people eat it raw, but it's very dangerous like that. It's easy to eat too much and, as a result, you end up so confused that suicide seems the only way out.'

He pulled a face. Why would anyone want to hallucinate? He thought back to the time when he was younger and had caught the most awful fever. He'd drifted in and out of consciousness non-stop and had hallucinated so badly that he'd been unable to tell what was a dream and what wasn't. Even the thought gave him a headache. 'So,' he said. 'Is it possible that he could have taken it?'

'There's nothing in his stomach contents to say so, as you already know. If it had been mixed in with the potion he had been taking, I would have recognised it.'

'You're saying no, then?' he pushed.

'I'm saying it's unlikely. However, I have seen one or two cases where it has been injected into the body.' She picked up an apron as she spoke, and took out her surgical gloves and put them on. 'I'll have a look at the body again and see if I can find any puncture marks that I didn't pick up the first time I examined it.'

She disappeared into the freezer room, the doors swinging behind her. Feeling suddenly curious, he walked over to her desk to see what she had been working on when he walked in. Her notebook was open, with the pen resting on the page she'd been writing on. He looked at it and chuckled. He hadn't realised her writing was so bad – at least he knew where his illegible scrawl came from. Still trying to work out what it said,

Thordric saw her come back into the room again, pushing the trolley with Kalljard's body on it.

'Now, Thordric, if you could...what are you doing?' she demanded.

'I...uh...nothing.'

'Come over here and help me. Put on a pair of those gloves there,' she said, indicating the box full of surgical gloves beside him. He opened it and pulled out a pair. They were made from a thin, waxy material that clung to his skin and made his fingers sweat. It was all he could do not to rip the things straight off again.

As he approached, his mother pulled back the white sheet covering the body. It looked exactly as it had done before, the skin sunken and the hair sparse.

'He looks the same as he did a week ago!' he said.

'Yes, that's because he's been frozen. Now, let's take a look here and see what we can find.'

She pulled back the sheet even more and instructed him to look over one side of the body, while she looked over the other. He wasn't sure what made him cringe more, the feeling of the gloves or the feel of Kalljard's skin. Whichever it was, his stomach decided to dance about violently.

It took them almost half an hour to check it thoroughly, but they couldn't find anything that might indicate he'd been injected. Thordric took off the gloves gratefully and sat down in a chair feeling rather weak.

'I was sure it'd been used on him,' he complained.

'Perhaps he was planning to use it in a new potion? As High Wizard, I'm sure he was involved in making some of the more useful potions that the council came up with.'

'How is a hallucination potion useful?' he asked. He felt almost as frail as when he had been learning magic at the house, only Lizzie wasn't there to give him any cake to help him recover.

'It's useful for the people who take *Winsome Sunbeam* whole – they would have a much easier way of measuring dosage then.'

Thordric shrugged and stood up, his legs wobbling underneath him. He had been staring at the mark above Kalljard's ear. That had been placed there by magic, but they still had no idea why. Perhaps...?

He bent down to look at it. The smell was fainter now, but distinct. If he removed the paint, then they would be able to see what, if anything, was underneath.

'Thordric? What are you up to now?' his mother asked, watching him closely.

'Only a little magic,' he said, grinning at her. Then he frowned. How *would* he remove it? With paint remover? It worked with normal paint, so a magic version should work with magic paint...shouldn't it? He tried it, and his mother's jaw dropped: it worked.

They bent in closer, to see what had been revealed. There was a small puncture mark, about the width of a needle. He felt rather smug.

'You know, Thordric, I'm starting to believe Lizzie was right about you. You have a lot of talent.' She smiled at him as she spoke, but he was crushed that she had doubted him at all. He turned away so she wouldn't see his eyes watering.

'What are you going to do now we've found it?' he asked, fighting back the thickness in his voice.

'I have to take a blood sample and then examine it to see if there are any traces of *Winsome Sunbeam*. It might take a while, so you should probably go back to the station.' She walked closer, noticing the slight trembling through his body. 'Thordric? Are you alright?'

'Yes,' he lied. 'It's just dead bodies make me feel uncomfortable after a while.'

Back at the station, after giving his report to the inspector, he asked for permission to work in one of the offices by himself. The inspector, surprisingly kindly, told him that they were all being used, so Thordric found himself on his way to Lizzie's town house instead. He hadn't expected to see her again so soon.

The snow was still thick on the ground, and the path he had to take was riddled with hidden ice. A few times he considered blasting it all away, but there were so many people about that he knew it would attract too much attention. Instead, he resolved to heat it up slightly so it became more sludge than ice.

As he came to Lizzie's garden, he found her outside, attempting to shift snow from the lawn. The shovel she was using was large and awkward, and her arms wobbled as she tried to lift it. Thordric shook his head. Keeping out of sight, he melted all the snow around her. She stood looking around, not quite sure what had happened. It was then that he decided to stroll out to meet her.

She didn't react quite how he'd expected, and he ended up with a large clump of mud on his cheek.

'Have you taken leave of your senses, boy?' she said, brandishing the shovel at him. He took a few involuntary steps backwards.

'I thought you would be impressed,' he said.

'Impressed? Of course I'm impressed. Impressed at how thick-headed you are. Come inside before someone walks past and sees what you've done!' she replied with exasperation.

He didn't argue. Following her inside, relishing in the warmth, he made his way to the kitchen. As usual, something delicious was cooking away on the stove and his stomach rumbled loudly. She tutted at him and brought out a bowl and plate, as well as a wet cloth to wipe his face on.

'Now that you're here, I suppose you'll expect to be fed,' she said, and ladled some thick stew into his bowl. She did the same for her own, and then cut up thick slices of bread for them to dip in it. 'There, that's better.' She sat down opposite him, but didn't eat.

'Thanks,' he said, hoping that was what she was waiting for him to say. It wasn't.

'Why did you feel it was necessary to use magic to clear my lawn, boy?'

'You looked like you needed help. There was no one about, I checked.'

'There is always someone about, boy. What's everyone to think when they walk past my house now? No amount of shovelling could clear away all that snow like you did.'

'Perhaps they'll just think it's a new spell from the council. Besides, why does it matter?' he asked, somewhat confused in her sudden change of attitude. 'You said that people would just have to accept that I can do magic, whether they like it or not.'

She sighed and interlaced her fingers. 'Yes, boy, I did. Just not yet. The council remains strong. They need to be shaken before you reveal yourself, otherwise they'll tread you down like everyone else.' She smiled then and began to eat. 'Now, tell me,' she said. 'Why are you here?'

He told her about the *Winsome Sunbeam* and the mirror in the High Wizard's chambers, and also about finding the puncture mark on Kalljard's body. Then he pulled out the paper he had taken from the desk. 'I also found this,' he said, wrinkling his nose at the smell it still gave off. He passed it to her, glad that the table was not anywhere near so long as the one in her other house.

She read it briefly. 'But this is just a new spell he needed to approve. What does this prove?'

'It's not a spell. Look at it closely,' he said.

She did. 'I can't see anything else on it.'

'Aren't the words blurred for you?' he asked, frowning.

'No. Should they be?'

'Yes. It's an illusion. And a strong one too. I couldn't remove it while I was there, so I took it with me. I was going to find an empty room at the station to try and remove it, but there wasn't one free. The inspector told me to come here instead.'

'I see,' she said, finishing her meal. 'Well, boy, you can stay as long as it takes.' She left the room, leaving him to work.

He pushed his bowl aside and looked at the paper. The blurring was even more evident now than it had been before. If Lizzie hadn't been able to see it, then it must be undetectable to people without magic.

He felt for the edges of the illusion again. It was slightly easier this time and he tugged hard at it. It didn't budge. He tried again, tugging firmly but slowly. Sweat broke out on his brow and his hands shook, but he had no luck.

Taking a deep breath, he stood up and walked around the room, before turning around and tugging at it quickly, as though trying to catch it by surprise. He tried it several times, each tug stronger than the last, but still the illusion stayed.

Cursing loudly, he levitated the paper and flung it against the wall. He peeled it off with his hands, from top to bottom.

The words were now so blurred that he couldn't make them out, but something was showing underneath.

With a sudden moment of clarity, he realised he'd been tugging at it from left to right, when it needed to be done from up to down. He tried it and, though the resistance was there, it was much weaker. With a few more tugs the illusion lifted.

He stared at the paper and gaped.

'Lizzie!' he shouted. 'Lizzie, come quick!'

She sped into the room, tripping over her skirts. 'What's the matter, boy? Are you hurt?'

He didn't answer, but shoved the paper into her hands. She read it, and her hand shot to her mouth. 'I think my brother needs to see this,' she managed weakly. He pulled a grim expression, words failing him.

They arrived at the station breathless, and Thordric had to let Lizzie lean on him as they went inside. He'd forgotten that she was almost twenty years older than his mother.

'Oi, oi, what's this then, small fry?' the constable at the reception desk asked him, eyeing Lizzie, who was quite unrecognisable with her hair having fallen down to her shoulders and her skirts in tatters. 'Bringing your dear grandmother to the station?

She did not take kindly to his remark. Standing up to her full height, she scooped back her hair, giving him such a stare that his eyes watered. 'Take me to my brother this instant, constable, or else I shall have you suspended indefinitely.'

'I, uh, begging your pardon, ma'am, I didn't realise...I'll take you right away!'

Lizzie barged into the inspector's office without knocking, with Thordric and the constable filing in behind her. The inspector raised his eyebrows and his moustache curled at the rude interruption. The constable garbled something unintelligible and fled from the room.

The inspector turned to Lizzie, but before he could speak, she thrust the paper at him.

'Take a look at this!' she said, her voice boiling. 'See what your precious Wizard Council was planning!'

15

THE INTERROGATIONS BEGIN

The inspector read what was on the paper. By the time he'd finished, half of his moustache had fallen out and his face was like chalk. 'I-I had no idea,' he said, his mouth agape. 'No idea whatsoever. W-where did this come from?'

'It was in the High Wizard's chambers,' Thordric said. 'It was disguised by magic.'

'Right then,' the inspector said, shaking slightly. 'Thordric, round up the constables and tell them I want to see them. Now, boy!'

Thordric left the office and called to all the constables at their desks, ignoring their jibes at him. They soon rounded up quickly when they found out that it was the inspector's orders. They gathered outside the office door, in time for the inspector and Lizzie to appear from within.

'Constables, I want all the Wizard Council arrested and brought here immediately!' the inspector bellowed. They all looked confused, and one brave man even called out.

'But Inspector, that's almost a thousand wizards!'

'Yes, constable, do you have an issue with that?'

'N-no, Inspector. It's just that our jail cells won't hold that many people.'

The inspector stopped short, his brow creasing so much that it looked like a miniature valley. 'Well then, only arrest the high-level Wizards – and Wizard Rarn!'

The constables hesitated.

'Use any means necessary but arrest them nonetheless, now MOVE!' the inspector roared.

They left in a hurry, not daring to test the inspector's patience a moment longer. The inspector put his hand to his brow and ordered Thordric to bring in tea and Jaffa cakes. He obliged, happy that the inspector was calling him by his real name again.

When he went into the office with the tray, the inspector and Lizzie were waiting for him expectantly. He poured them both tea and took up the inspector's offer to have some himself. 'Do you think you can handle interrogations, boy?' the inspector asked him as he sat down.

'Interrogations, Inspector?' Thordric said, burning his mouth on his tea.

'Yes, boy...interrogations. Even with just the high-level wizards here, that's going to be thirty men we have to talk to. I want to find out exactly how far *this*,' he said, furiously waving the piece of paper, 'has gone down the ranks, and I'll need your help.' He sat back in his chair, looking suddenly weary. 'You were right all along, Lizzie...so was Patrick. I'm so very sorry I never believed him, or you.'

The constables trickled back within the hour, dragging wizards of all sizes and ages with them, who were shouting and screaming at the terrible injustice of it all. Wizard Rarn was one of the last to be brought in, along with High Wizard Vey, who strolled in as calmly as if he were having his hair trimmed at the local barbers. Wizard Rarn was not nearly as composed, particularly when he saw Thordric making notes as he watched from the sidelines. 'You!' he screamed. 'How *dare* you arrest us? How *dare* you arrest his reverence?'

'Hush, Rarn. I doubt the good inspector and young Thordric here would have done it if they hadn't good reason to,' Vey said. He motioned for Thordric to carry on, and let the constables take him to the cells.

The office door opened behind Thordric, and the inspector came out with Lizzie. 'Boy, I have to be going now,' she said. 'Please help my brother as much as you can.'

'I'll do my best,' Thordric said and, turning away from her, he and the inspector went down to the cells themselves. The constables who had taken all the wizards there were resting on the steps, panting heavily, and more than a few of them sported vibrant new hair colours and distorted features. The inspector raised an eyebrow, but said nothing other than for them to help themselves to tea and Jaffa cakes.

High Wizard Vey had been given a cell all to himself at the request of the other wizards. He was sitting on the bench, his eyes closed and occasionally waving a hand whenever one of them tried to do or say something nasty.

Thordric noticed with a grin that Vey's simple hand wave had also put Wizard Rarn into a deep sleep to stop his incessant shouting, much to everyone's delight.

The inspector stood in front of the cells, staring at them all coolly. His temper had calmed now and he was able to assess the situation with a professional eye. 'Wizards of the council, you are here because I have uncovered evidence of a plot most foul. A plot orchestrated by the late High Wizard Kalljard himself.'

The wizards stared at him, and Vey opened one of his eyes.

'My assistant and I will be interrogating you all to see how deeply this plot ran, and if necessary, deal the appropriate discipline,' the inspector continued. He turned to Thordric. 'You take the youngsters. I'll take the older ones.'

'What about Vey?' Thordric whispered.

'I think we should both interrogate him,' he replied. He beckoned to two constables still hanging around, and asked them to escort one of the younger wizards to the smaller interview room with Thordric, while he took one of the oldest wizards into the larger room himself.

The wizard who Thordric had to interrogate first happened to be the one who'd served them food when they had dined with Vey. He was a nervous young man, and Thordric would never have guessed that he was a high-level wizard. He hardly looked much older than Thordric himself, though he suspected that he must be if Lizzie was right about how long their training took.

'You're...you're the one who dined with his reverence before he was elected, aren't you?' he asked Thordric once they were seated.

'Yes, I am,' Thordric replied, intending to say more, but then it suddenly occurred to him that he didn't have the foggiest idea of where to start.

'How long have you been part of the council?' he asked, after a *long* silence.

The wizard fiddled with the sleeves of his robes. 'Just over six months, sir, right after I finished my training,' he replied.

Thordric was surprised. 'How did you make it to the high level after only six months, then?' he asked.

'I was only promoted a few days ago, sir, at his reverence's request. He had seen me cast a growth spell on the trees in the garden. I wasn't supposed to touch them without permission, so I thought he might punish me, but he didn't. He made me keeper of the garden instead, a title only usually given to high-level wizards. Some of my fellows complained about it, so he promoted me to stop them fussing.'

'I see,' Thordric said. He wracked his brain for another question, not wanting to jump in directly with the one about the plot. 'Er, how well did you know High Wizard Kalljard?'

'I didn't, sir. I only saw him the once, when he accepted me as part of the council. He didn't pay me much mind though, since there were five of us inducted on the same day.'

Thordric sighed. This was going nowhere.

'Were you aware that High Wizard Kalljard was planning to kill off all the half-wizards in the country?' he said coldly.

'He *what*? No, sir, that can't be true! The late High Wizard disliked half-wizards, but he would never seek to kill them. Why would he? They can't do any harm.'

'Perhaps he felt that their magic might in fact be as strong as yours,' Thordric said, watching the wizard closely.

'What do you mean? Half-wizards can't use their magic. It always goes wrong.'

'So everyone says.' Thordric stood up. This young wizard had known nothing. He wasn't guilty of anything, except perhaps having a terrible sense of style, given his odd choice of bright pink and brown coloured robes. Thordric asked the constables to take him back to the cells and bring in the next one.

A few minutes later, the constables came back with a wizard so tall his head touched the ceiling, and a large amount of muscle bulged out from under his robes, contrasting oddly with his scraggly black beard and long hair. His expression wasn't pleasant. They seated him in from of Thordric, who cleared his throat, trying to ignore the intense loathing that oozed across the table at him.

Nervously he looked across at the constables, but they were

standing well back, about as useful as a pair of old boots. Sitting up straight, he began asking questions. He started out the same way, asking how long the wizard had been part of the council. No reply. He asked again, but still, no reply. He moved on, but didn't so much as get a blink out of the wizard.

Time passed by and Thordric knew he had to make him talk. He decided to change tact. 'What do you think of half-wizards?' he asked.

The muscle-bound wizard laughed, a low rumbling sound rather like thunder. 'Half-wizards are no more than a disgrace to wizard kind. A bumbling collection of fools who think that just because their fathers were wizards, they can do magic too. Hardly worth a moment's thought.'

Thordric made a fist under the table, trying not to let his anger show. 'So,' he said, keeping his voice in check. 'If there was a plan to purge the country of them, would you agree to it?'

'Of course I would. They deserve to be locked up somewhere out of sight,' the wizard said, folding his arms. His biceps bulged, making his sleeves tighten so much that they might tear.

'Locked away? Is that all? Wouldn't you want them dead?' Thordric pressed, raising his eyebrow.

'Dead?' the wizard said, taken aback. 'Never! I admit that I don't like them, and they certainly don't deserve any respect, but I wouldn't want them dead! What kind of person would wish that on them?'

'*Your* late High Wizard, for one.'

'His reverence Kalljard? How dare you? That's absurd!' the wizard said loudly, half standing.

'Sit down, sir. We're not finished here yet.' Thordric choked on the sudden authority in his voice. He seemed to be enjoying himself. The wizard sat down hard, making the chair groan underneath him.

'Do you have any evidence of this plot?' the wizard

demanded, his muscles bulging threateningly. Thordric ignored it. He fished through his pockets again and produced one of the copies of the paper that the inspector had instructed him to make. He pushed it across the table to the wizard.

'Where did you get this?' he demanded, his eyes wide and muscles now sagging.

'The High Wizard's chambers, before High Wizard Vey transferred his belongings. It was lying on the desk. That is the late High Wizard Kalljard's handwriting, is it not?' Thordric asked, realising that no one had actually confirmed it yet.

'It is...I used to carry notes between departments for him. He never sealed them...'

'And did any of them suggest how foul a wizard he really was?' Thordric said.

'No, young sir,' the wizard said, dropping all his remaining aggressiveness. 'There was nothing to suggest this...this *foulness* of mind.' Thordric signalled to the constables to take him away, but the wizard stayed in his chair. 'If anyone knew about it...I suppose that would have been incentive enough to kill him, wouldn't it?'

'I don't know, but it certainly wouldn't help anyone's case,' Thordric said slowly. The wizard sighed deeply and stood up, holding out his arms for the constables to lead him away. Thordric got up and stretched, wincing as the feeling came back into his buttocks. There was a knock on the door, and he opened it to find the inspector there.

'Hold the interrogations for a moment, boy. You mother is here with some interesting news.'

He followed the inspector back up to his office, where his mother was already waiting. She had straightened her hair since last time he'd seen her, and from the rose petal aroma around her, she'd sprayed on some perfume too. 'Ah, there you are, Thordric,' she said as he entered. 'I've finished analysing Kalljard's blood. It seems that our theory was correct.'

'He was injected with *Winsome Sunbeam*?'

'Yes,' she said, straightening up. The inspector sat down with a fresh pot of tea, and poured her a cup. She gave him a smile that made Thordric think he might vomit.

'There is one thing, though. The amount in his blood wouldn't have been sufficient to drive him mad enough to kill himself, only to make him see things that were slightly out of the ordinary.'

'So, we still don't know what actually killed him?' the inspector said, picking up a Jaffa cake.

'No, there's nothing conclusive,' she said.

'What about the mirror we found?' Thordric said, deciding to show off and pour himself some tea by magic. The inspector swallowed his Jaffa cake whole.

'What do you mean, boy?' he said, coughing so much his eyes watered.

'If you were imagining things and looked in a mirror, wouldn't it be possible to confuse yourself with someone else?' Thordric said.

The inspector looked at him as though seeing him properly for the first time. 'You know, boy, that's a jolly good theory! Would that be possible, Maggie?'

'Very possible. Yet I don't see why that would make him attack himself.'

Thordric looked from her to the inspector. The inspector shifted uncomfortably in his chair. 'Haven't you told her yet, Inspector?'

16

A CONVINCING DISGUISE

'Well,' his mother said, swallowing. 'Given those circumstances, he would likely have been very para-noid. Giving him *Winsome Sunbeam* would only have made it worse.'

She trembled, and looked at Thordric as though she couldn't bear to lose him. He felt his face grow hot. If his theory was true, then it wasn't a case of outright murder. Someone had set it all up so that Kalljard would kill himself. Now he knew the truth, he couldn't help but sympathise with whoever had done it.

High Wizard Kalljard, head of the Wizard Council, was the most important person in the country aside from the royal family. Nearly everyone had respected and revered him, igno-rant of the monster that he really was. Now they would *all* know the truth.

Thordric had no doubt now that Kalljard had been the one to kill Lizzie's husband, if not personally, then by directing another. Who knew how many other half-wizards he had already disposed of before drawing up the official plans they'd found?

He got up from his chair, ready to continue with the interrogations, but then turned to his mother, having a sudden thought. 'Is there a way to prove he killed himself?'

The inspector and Thordric's mother looked at each other and then slowly shook their heads. 'This is the world of magic, boy,' the inspector said. 'Unless you can find a way to prove it with magic, then we have no way of knowing for sure. Except if someone confesses, of course.'

'Lizzie didn't teach me any spells for killing people, so there's no way I can tell...wait a moment!' His mouth spread into a grin as he realised what the idea was that'd been circling about in his mind. 'Inspector, I've interrogated two wizards so far, and I believe both are innocent of Kalljard's death and of his plotting. Why not let *them* examine the body and see if they can tell us what happened?'

The inspector stood up too, eye to eye with Thordric. 'I have to say, I would fully encourage your plan...if it wasn't for the small detail that the entire Wizard Council believes we buried him days ago.'

Thordric slumped down again. 'Then we're never going to know what happened.'

It was his mother's turn to speculate. She smoothed down her hair and looked at them both. 'What if the body is disguised?' she said. 'We could say it was another half-wizard who tried to experiment.'

'They'll know if I use magic to disguise it. It gives off too strong a smell,' Thordric complained.

'Not everything has to be done by magic, Thordric. Inspector, send a constable to fetch your sister, I could use her help with this,' she said. She got up and breezed out of the door, hardly sparing them a glance goodbye.

Thordric and the inspector sat in silence for a moment.

'They'll see through a normal disguise too, if it's anything like her fancy dress costumes,' Thordric muttered.

The inspector heard him, and with one smooth movement, smacked him on the side of his head with one of the books that had been lying on the desk. 'Have some faith in your mother, boy, she's very skilled.' Thordric raised an eyebrow at this, but the inspector ignored it and called in a constable to go and fetch Lizzie. Then he and Thordric made their way back down to the interview rooms to deal with the next batch of wizards.

Three or four wizards later, all of whom had known nothing, there was another tap on the interview room door. It was a constable with a message from Thordric's mother.

'The pathologist wishes you to know that everything is ready, small fry,' the constable said.

Thordric ignored the jape. 'Tell her I shall be there momentarily,' he replied. He turned back to the current wizard he was interrogating, and calmly told him of Kalljard's plot, ready for the usual shocked reaction. He wasn't disappointed.

When he was done, he made his way back to the cells and requested the two wizards he had interviewed first – the young gardener and the bearded muscle-bound one. They'd been sent up to wait in one of the offices in case they told the others about Kalljard's plot.

By the time he got there, the tiny office was crammed full of wizards, for the inspector's ones had been sent there too. He squeezed his way in and managed to stand on a chair so he could see all their faces. The ones he wanted were at the back, on different sides of the room. He called for them to come with him, feeling terribly rude for not knowing their names.

They came without a fuss, quieted by the revelation that

Kalljard had been truly monstrous and they walked silently next to Thordric all the way to the morgue. When they got there, they found Lizzie and his mother both dressed in white aprons and surgical gloves, standing around the body on the table. Thordric tried not to show his surprise at how different it looked.

Kalljard's beard and hair had been trimmed and coloured a deep red, and they had put various tattoos on his arms and chest, somehow making them look as though they had been there for years. Even Thordric found it hard to recognise him. The skin was still sunken and leathery though, which was what he'd wanted the wizards to see. It had been safe to bring these two, as he knew they hadn't seen the body at all and thus wouldn't have recognised the condition it was in.

'Good evening, gentlemen,' his mother said. 'I have requested your presence here to help me with the post-mortem on this poor fellow.'

The two wizards glanced at each other. 'We-we would be g-glad to help,' the younger one said.

Thordric's mother smiled. 'Excellent. Now, as you can see, the poor man has suffered some form of extreme dehydration and decomposition.' She paused, indicating the state of the skin. 'We knew he was a half-wizard, and so have presumed that he was trying to use his own magic and, as always, it back-fired on him. But I need to be certain of that so I can confirm it in my report. I need you two gentlemen to help me discover what the true cause was.'

'I-I see,' the young wizard said. He looked closely at the body. 'I-I would say that your th-theory was c-correct, madam. Would you agree, Wizard Myak?' he said, turning to the tall wizard. The tall wizard leant in too, and extended a finger to prod the body several times.

'I do indeed, Wizard Batsu,' he said gruffly. 'Although this is very strong magic indeed. Are you sure he was only a half-wizard?'

'It's what I was told, sir,' Thordric's mother said, without a hint of concern.

'Then he could have been a Wanderer. That would be a more logical explanation, since I do not believe the magic of a simple half-wizard could do this much damage. No, this man was a Wanderer.'

'How is it you can tell, sir?' Lizzie said, stepping in. She looked Wizard Myak in the eye, commanding an answer.

'Wanderers are deserters from the Wizard Council Training Facility,' he replied, staring at her with equal intensity. 'As such, they are highly trained wizards, capable of everything that the members of the Wizard Council are. If I am correct, then the spell this man used required a high level of training, and is notoriously hard to control. Only high-level wizards such as myself can control spells like that, although we never use them. They are for defensive purposes only.'

'Then, based on that, you could equally say that a member of the council such as yourself might have used it on him in a defensive situation?' Thordric challenged.

Wizard Myak flexed his muscles, but Wizard Batsu cut in before he could do anything.

'Ah, no, actually. Th-there is a rule that any wizard who uses high-level defensive spells must report them and go in front of the High Wizard to state the reason why it was used. No one has had to do that in over fifty years. Check our records if you like.'

'What if someone just didn't report it?' Thordric pushed.

'We-we are bound by o-oath—' Wizard Batsu started.

'But that is not your problem,' rumbled Wizard Myak. 'Your problem is that this spell would not have killed him. Made him weak, yes, but not killed him.'

Thordric deflated. If that wasn't what killed him, then what was? He squeezed his lips together, trying not to say the long list of curse words streaming into his mind. He had gotten absolutely nowhere. 'Do you have any idea what did?' he said at length.

'No, young sir,' Wizard Myak said. 'I do not.'

'Nor-nor I,' Wizard Batsu added.

Thordric took them back to the station, where he saw several more wizards had been filed into the cramped office. The inspector certainly was going through them at a fast pace. He left them there and went down to the cells, where only a dozen or so remained. He spoke to the constable standing guard and asked him to get the inspector for him. The constable hesitated, but Thordric saw High Wizard Vey make a small motion with his hand and the constable soon hurried off.

'Why did you do that?' Thordric asked Vey, walking closer to the cells so he didn't have to shout. The other wizards watched him and Wizard Rarn, now awake, muttered something dark under his breath.

'I thought I'd help you out. The inspector has given you a hard job here, Thordric, expecting his men to follow the orders of what they believe to be a mere boy. They should respect you, clearly you are very insightful and intelligent – a quality, I fear, that most of them do not possess.'

Thordric couldn't help grinning. 'I'm sorry we had to lock you up like this, Vey,' he said.

Wizard Rarn riled at this. 'Show his reverence the proper respect, boy!' he shouted. 'He is High Wizard, and you would do well to remember that!'

Vey looked at him and raised an eyebrow, then with one small surge of magic put him to sleep again. 'I'm afraid Wizard

Rarn cares too much about status and official procedure. Personally, I find my title a little tiresome.'

Thordric would have liked to have spoken to Vey for a bit longer, but the constable appeared again with the inspector behind him, the remains of his moustache curling out in all directions. 'Inspector, I need to speak with you privately,' Thordric said quickly, before he was shouted at.

They went back up to the inspector's office, not bothering with tea this time. The inspector stood up behind his chair, too agitated to sit. 'I hope you've got good news, boy. I'm not getting anything out of those wizards.'

Thordric took a deep breath, and told him what Wizard Myak and Wizard Batsu had said. When he finished, the inspector was silent. He sat down and opened his drawer, taking out a small, ornate glass bottle, filled with a blue green swirly liquid. He placed it on the desk in front of Thordric. Thordric licked his lips nervously.

'Do you know what this is, boy?' he said, indicating the bottle.

'A-a potion, Inspector?'

'Yes. It helps to calm my nerves after a long day. Have you any idea who might have given it to me?'

'No, Inspector,' he replied, wondering where the conversation was going.

The inspector looked down, rather sadly. 'It was given to me by High Wizard Kalljard, the day he came to congratulate me on my promotion to Inspector. That was the first time I had met him and I would have sworn then that he was the most generous and understanding person I had ever met. Twenty cases, he gave to me. Enough to last me from then to well into my retirement.'

'Does it work, Inspector?'

'Yes. Too well, sometimes.' He paused, shaking his head.

'Lizzie told you about her husband, didn't she? About how I hushed up his death so that the papers wouldn't go after her?'

'She...she did,' he said, as goose pimples rose on his arms. What was the inspector getting at?

'It all happened not long after I'd first been given this and I took it every day. It dulled my good sense, Thordric. Made me ignore protocol in favour of casting the well-known stereotype of half-wizards. If I hadn't been taking it, I would have done my job properly and found out what really happened that night when he left the house.'

He picked the bottle up and smashed it, making Thordric jump.

'Help me find out who set up Kalljard's death, boy, so I can personally thank them for ridding this world of someone so despicable.'

17

INTERVIEWING RARN

Wizard Rarn sat in front of Thordric, breathing heavily and fiddling with the sleeves of his robes. Any shred of his polite demeanour that he had shown the first time Thordric went with the inspector to the council was gone. Now he was snide and uncooperative, as Thordric had found out over the past half-hour.

'Rarn, I will get you to tell me what you know,' Thordric said. He wished the inspector had taken on Rarn, but since he was one of the younger wizards it had fallen to Thordric to interrogate him.

'My title is Wizard Rarn, insolent boy!' Rarn shouted.

'Fine. *Wizard* Rarn, you will answer all of my questions. Now, how long have you been a member of the Wizard Council?'

'What concern is that of yours?' Rarn said.

'Answer me!' Thordric shouted, jumping up to his feet. 'Or I will tell the inspector that you need to be incarcerated for life.'

Rarn glared and ran his hand down along the table, scratching it with his nails. The high-pitched noise it made had

Thordric gritting his teeth and tensing every muscle. 'Very well,' Rarn hissed. 'I've been a member of the Wizard Council for ten years.'

'And what level are you?' Thordric asked, flattening his hair down.

Rarn flared his nostrils. 'I am a middle-level wizard, though High Wizard Kalljard hinted that I would be promoted several times.'

'But he was killed before he could do it?'

'Obviously, imbecile. I am sure his reverence will go forth with it once he has become accustomed to his office.'

Thordric almost burst out laughing. High Wizard Vey, promote *him*? Never. Thordric knew Vey had more sense than that. 'How well did you know High Wizard Kalljard then?'

'Well enough that he personally chose me to clean his chambers every day. I dusted all his bookshelves and changed his bed sheets and I arranged his robes for the next day—'

'So, you had complete access?'

'Of course. How else would I have completed my duties?' Rarn said.

'Did you ever notice a mirror in there?' Thordric asked. Rarn raised his eyebrows and fiddled with his sleeves again.

'There was a mirror,' he said. 'But it was taken away a few days before the...incident occurred. I believe it was replaced by a wardrobe.'

Now Thordric was getting somewhere. If Rarn knew who had supposedly moved it, then he would be one step closer to solving the case. He asked if Rarn did know, but he said he'd been terribly unwell that day and hadn't been there to supervise. Thordric found that awfully suspicious, but Rarn gave the names of six wizards he shared a dormitory with who could confirm what he said.

Keeping Rarn in the interview room, Thordric went to find

a constable to send down to the council building to confirm his alibi. Being of only middle-level skills, none of the wizards currently bunched up in the spare office knew Rarn that well, so they were of no help.

While he was waiting, he doubled the security outside the interview room he was using and went along to the larger one where the inspector was still interrogating the older wizards. There was a small window which he could look through to see how things were going. The old man currently in there was in tears. Thordric didn't have to guess why.

The man wiped his eyes with the end of his beard, but the tears kept on coming. The inspector pressed him for details, asking if he had known anything about the plot, but the man simply shook his head, unable to speak. The inspector sighed and got up, signalling for the constables on guard to take the wizard upstairs. He caught sight of Thordric and came out to see him.

'I thought you were dealing with Rarn, boy,' he said, pulling at his moustache. More of it had come out since last time and it no longer seemed to have its own persona.

'I am, Inspector. He didn't co-operate at first, but I told him you'd lock him up for life if he didn't start talking.'

The inspector chuckled. 'You're starting to show some promise, boy. So, what did he say when you loosened his tongue?'

'He told me he was Kalljard's personal chamber cleaner. Supposedly, Kalljard picked him out personally for the job.'

'He was a chambermaid?' The inspector laughed so hard that his eyes watered.

'There's more, Inspector. Rarn saw the mirror in Kalljard's chambers, but he said it had been taken out and replaced with a wardrobe a few days before the incident.'

'Oh, did he now? Where was he when this happened?'

'He claims he was unwell that day and stayed in the dormitories. I've sent a constable there to check with the other wizards to confirm his alibi.'

'That's good work, boy. Keep at it and let me know what else the slimy git says.' He turned to go back in. 'Oh, by the way, boy. You've got some whiskers growing; it'll be time for your first shave soon, I think.' He pointed at Thordric's stubbly chin.

Thordric's cheeks started to redden, but the inspector had gone before he could notice.

He walked back to the interview room where Rarn was and looked through the window to make sure he wasn't up to anything. Rarn saw Thordric and gave him a long, flat stare. Thordric turned his back on him and went upstairs to wait for the constable to come back.

He made himself some tea and even dared to take a few of the inspector's Jaffa cakes. Sitting down at an empty desk, he looked out of the window. It was dark now, and was snowing again. He hoped the constable he'd sent came back soon, for otherwise Thordric would be working into the night trying to get more information out of Rarn.

Noticing the wizards in the office all staring at him, he asked the constable to dismiss them. There was no point in keeping them here if they really did know nothing. High Wizard Vey would have to stay the night though, as he would be the last to be interrogated. Thordric yawned and drained his teacup, just in time for the constable to walk in the door. He looked as though he would freeze at any second. Thordric poured him some tea and he took it gratefully.

'T-they a-all c-confirmed i-it,' he said, his teeth chattering.

Thordric cursed silently. 'Thank you, Constable,' he said, and directed him towards the single fireplace. He watched as the poor man took off his wet jacket and huddled up as close to the flames as possible without burning himself. Thordric gave a nod and then descended the steps back down to the interview room.

Rarn was grinning smugly and had turned his previously red robe to a dark blue. It made his pale face look unwell. Thordric found that he loathed the man. He picked up his chair and moved it right next to where Rarn was sitting, close enough to throttle him if need be.

'Wizard Rarn, when the inspector first went to pay his respects to High Wizard Kalljard, I believe you told him your theory on how he died. Remind me what it was,' he said coolly.

Rarn straightened himself. 'I said that I believed he had stopped taking his everlasting youth potion,' he said, levelling with Thordric's gaze.

'Then what if I were to tell you that we found potion in High Wizard Kalljard's stomach, and it matched the potion he had been ever so careful to hide inside one of his bed posts. If he had truly stopped taking it, then there would have been none left in his body.'

'And who is to say that the one you found in his room was indeed his everlasting youth potion?' Rarn said, licking his lips. 'I bet the potion you found was bright pink, wasn't it?'

Thordric frowned. 'What makes you say that?'

Rarn laughed. 'It was no secret what colour his youth potion was; he drank it in the dining halls several times.' He turned to Thordric slyly. 'Do you know how many potions there are that happen to be bright pink? I know of at least five, each with *very* different properties,' he said, his voice oozing with venom.

Thordric had had enough. He banged his fist down on the table, resisting the urge to levitate Rarn into the wall. No, he thought, I need him conscious.

Instead, he left the room quickly, and sprinted through the

station and out the door. He sped towards the morgue, hoping that his mother and Lizzie were still there. They were.

As he approached them, he saw they were deep in conversation, but they stopped abruptly as they caught the look of contempt on his face.

'Thordric?' his mother began. 'Is everything alright?'

He shook his head and put his hands up, knowing that if he spoke, he would say something he would regret. Instead, he rushed over to his mother's desk, rummaging through all the vials until he found what he was looking for. There! He picked up the bottle of pink liquid they'd found in Kalljard's bedpost and then ran back out faster than any gale-storm wind could blow.

On his way, he ran straight into the inspector.

'Inspector,' Thordric said, trying not to let his anger affect his speech. 'I think you might want to come with me.'

The inspector opened his mouth to protest, but he caught the urgency in Thordric's eyes. 'Very well then, boy,' he said and let Thordric take him into the interview room that Rarn was in.

Thordric thrust the potion at Rarn. 'Drink it,' he spat. 'Drink it and we'll find out what it does.'

Rarn stood and backed up against the wall. He was eyeing the potion as if it were poison. 'Now, there's no need to be hasty,' he said, holding up his hands. 'It was simply a theory, after all. You asked what I thought...'

'What's this all about, boy?' the inspector said, rounding on Thordric.

'This slippery slime-ball suggested that someone had switched Kalljard's youth potion with a different one of the same colour. I wanted to test that theory.'

'Oh,' the inspector said, glancing from Thordric to Rarn. 'Well, I suppose we don't really have another way of testing it.'

He looked at Rarn, the corners of his mouth sliding upwards. 'I'm terribly sorry, my dear Wizard Rarn,' he said sarcastically. 'But I'm afraid you'll have to do as the boy says.' He stepped to the side, becoming a spectator, and let Thordric continue.

Thordric forcibly put the bottle into Rarn's hand. Rarn didn't move. 'I didn't want you to find out so soon, but you leave me no choice,' Thordric said. He poured his magic into Rarn's hands, making him undo the bottle and pour its contents down his throat.

As Rarn drank, he looked at Thordric with a mix of terror and surprise in his eyes, and a puddle of yellow liquid appeared around his feet.

'Looks like you'll need clean robes, too,' the inspector chuckled.

Thordric crossed his arms and waited. He waited for half an hour, then an hour. Nothing happened. Rarn still stood, in perfect health, staring at Thordric.

'It seems you're in luck, Wizard Rarn,' the inspector said, the sound of the clock upstairs striking midnight rousing him from his doze. 'Your theory seems to have been wrong.'

Rarn let out a whimper of relief. The inspector beckoned Thordric over and whispered in his ear. Thordric turned back to Rarn, a satisfied grimace on his face and levitated him out of the room and back along the corridor to the holding cells.

As he passed, High Wizard Vey raised an eyebrow at him, but didn't look overly surprised. Thordric put Rarn in the empty cell next to him.

'Don't think I'm done with you yet,' he said. Rarn whimpered again and scrambled as far away from Thordric as he could.

'I'm afraid we can't interview you until tomorrow, Vey,' he said, turning to him. 'I'm very sorry to say that you'll have to stay here for the night. Are you warm enough? Would like some extra blankets or something to eat or drink?'

'I'm fine, thank you, Thordric. There's no need to apologise, I'm sure you've had a long day.' Thordric nodded and said goodbye, walking up the cold steps back to the main station room. He met his mother coming out of the morgue, and they walked home together. This time Thordric made no secret of his powers and melted all the snow in the street so they could stroll along more easily.

18

IDENTITY REVEALED

Thordric's sleep was restless that night, and there were times when he wasn't sure if he was awake or not. He felt terribly warm despite the coolness of the house and arose two hours earlier than normal.

He stood in front of his wash basin, wide awake. The stubble on his chin really had grown, and with a slight grimace he picked up the razor his mother had given him for his birthday the previous year. It was menacingly sharp, making his Adam's apple quiver simply looking at it.

Nearly half an hour later, with spots of tissue paper covering his face where he'd nicked the skin, he stood clean shaven. Unfortunately, he'd been so nervous doing it that he was now drenched in sweat and had to have a bath. He went outside to the bathhouse, wincing as the chill wind bit at him, and pulled down the tin bath from the wall. He placed it in the middle of the small room and then grabbed the buckets to fetch the water with. Going back and forth to the kitchen, he filled the bath until it was as full as he could get it. It was quicker than usual, for he no longer had to heat it up on the stove first.

He used his magic, as he had done at Lizzie's house, and laughed at the trouble he'd had with it back then.

He jumped in, relaxing as the wonderfully warm water lapped at his skin. By the time he got out, it was time for him to dress in his uniform and leave for the station, with enough left to bolt down the porridge his mother had made.

When he got to the station, he found all the constables looking wearier than he'd ever felt and, when the inspector walked out of his office, he had to struggle to control his face. The remainder of the inspector's moustache had fallen out and his eyes were so dark it looked as though he'd borrowed Thordric's mother's eye kohl and smudged it all around them.

'Morning, boy,' he grumbled, letting out an involuntary yawn. 'Rarn's waiting in the interview room for you. He's as terrified as he was once you'd finished with him last night. Shouldn't be any trouble today. Come and get me once you're done and we'll speak to High Wizard Vey together.'

'I will, Inspector,' he said. Then, as an afterthought, he leant in to the inspector's ear, keeping his voice low so that none of the constables would be able to hear. 'Er, Inspector, I can, er, grow your moustache back for you if you want.'

The inspector leant back in surprise. 'Really?' he whispered. 'You can actually do that? In that case, boy, you'd better step into my office for a few moments.' He looked around at the constables, but they seemed too tired to have taken any interest.

Thordric followed him into the office and closed the door behind them. 'How long do you want it, Inspector?' he asked.

The inspector shrugged. 'As long as it was before it started falling out, and as thick, too.'

'Alright, then,' Thordric said. 'Pardon me, Inspector.' He put his fingers under the inspector's nose, pouring his magic into his hand and miming pulling the hair forth from the skin. It appeared slowly, sparse at first, but once Thordric found the balance of magic he had to use, it grew fuller. Hardly a minute had passed before the inspector had his moustache back, as bushy and emotionally responsive as before.

'That's very impressive, boy,' the inspector said, running his fingers through it. 'I believe that's cause to give you a raise.'

Thordric grinned and left the inspector grooming his moustache with his comb. He went downstairs, past the cells where he saw Vey eating some freshly baked bread and cheese for breakfast, then into the interview room. Rarn was crouching miserably in one corner, ignoring the table and chairs completely. Thordric decided to help him, levitating him into the chair and forcing him to sit up straight.

'Good morning, Rarn,' Thordric said, sitting down himself. Rarn tried to push his chair further back, but Thordric held it in place.

'What...what are you?' Rarn managed. His robes started changing colour, going from blue to purple to red and through the rest of the colours of the rainbow. He didn't seem to realise he was doing it.

'I'm a half-wizard,' Thordric replied calmly. Rarn looked sceptical.

'But you're able to use magic without causing damage. You can't be a half-wizard. They're not strong enough.'

'I *am* a half-wizard, Rarn. I've just had training in magic like you have.'

'From whom? Who would dare share our secrets with one of your kind?'

'That is none of your concern. Now, let me ask you a question. Have you ever seen this?' he pushed the copy of Kalljard's plot over to him. Rarn glanced at it and shrugged.

'I may have. It looks like all the other documents High Wizard Kalljard had on his desk,' he sniffed.

'Read it, Rarn,' Thordric said, tilting Rarn forwards so that he had no choice but to look at the paper properly. Rarn read it and shrugged again. 'You knew about it, didn't you?' Thordric accused.

'Yes, I knew. But what concern of mine was it if that's what High Wizard Kalljard was planning?'

Thordric lost his temper again. 'What concern was it of yours?' he bellowed. 'You would have let him kill innocent people?'

'But he didn't believe they were innocent. He wouldn't have believed *you* were innocent either. I would not have dared to say otherwise.'

'You should have told your brethren. They would have been brave enough to do so had they have known.'

'Oh no, I don't believe they would have. You see, High Wizard Kalljard had them all drinking that same potion your Inspector is so fond of. They wouldn't have been able to say anything against him even if they'd wanted to.'

'You better not be lying, Rarn,' Thordric said, gritting his teeth.

'Why should I lie?' Rarn smirked. 'Ask his reverence if you don't believe me. He used to make it all for them.'

Thordric toyed with the idea of making all of Rarn's hair fall out, but he couldn't bear to hear the man whimper pathetically again. 'One more question, Rarn. Who killed Kalljard and how was it done?'

Rarn made a face, as though Thordric had dealt him a nasty insult. 'I assure you, I have absolutely no idea.'

'Fine,' Thordric said. He got up and let the constables take Rarn back to the cells, and went to find the inspector again.

When he got upstairs, he found that the inspector had left a note for him saying to find him at the morgue. He made his way there, wondering if it was purely for instructions or whether his mother had discovered something else.

Lizzie was with them when he got there; they were deep in discussion while huddled around a large, weathered-looking book.

'Inspector, you wished to see me?'

'Ah, there you are, boy,' he said, turning around. 'Come here and take a look at this.'

Thordric went to them and lent over the book. It was on a page titled 'Minerals for overall health'. The inspector tapped at an entry called *Ink Eye Pyrite*.

'*Ink Eye Pyrite*?' Thordric asked, puzzled.

'Yes,' his mother said. 'Do you remember there was a mineral in the potion Kalljard had been taking that I didn't recognise? Well, that's it.'

'Er, great,' he said, unsure of why they thought this was significant.

'It's more than great, Thordric,' she continued. 'I knew Lizzie here had some of her husband's old books, and as well as being capable of serious magic like you, he was also something of a geologist. I asked her if she could bring some here to help me identify what it was and here it is.'

'I still don't...'

'Read what it says, boy,' Lizzie chided. He did.

Ink Eye Pyrite (Ousus Inkett): Commonly found in mountainous regions and near volcanoes. Deep red with silver and blue flecks, it is a soft mineral with many healing properties, including increased energy and overall well-being. Note: if used with certain herbs, it can prove to be fatal.

. . .

'If used with certain herbs it can be fatal?' he asked, looking up.

'Indeed,' his mother said. 'But none of the herbs used in the potion have that effect. However...'

'The *Winsome Sunbeam* did, didn't it?' Thordric asked, suddenly catching on.

'Correct,' she said.

'So, if we find out who injected him with that, we have our killer?'

'Precisely, boy,' the inspector said. 'Now, what did Rarn have to say for himself?'

Thordric blinked. He had completely forgotten about Rarn. 'He knew about the plot, Inspector,' he said.

The inspector's newly grown moustache curled.

'There's more,' Thordric continued. 'He told me that Kall-jard was making the other wizards drink the same potion he gave you. Even if they had known about the plot, they wouldn't have attempted to try and stop him.'

'He really was a monster, wasn't he?' his mother said. Thordric, Lizzie, and the inspector all nodded.

'Did he say anything else?' the inspector asked.

'Well, he said he didn't know who the killer was...and he also said to ask High Wizard Vey about the potion they were all taking. Apparently, Vey was the one who brewed it for them.'

'I think we should go and have a talk with him then, after all we've kept him waiting long enough,' the inspector said. 'Would you care to join us, ladies? It may prove to be a rather interesting conversation.'

Lizzie and Thordric's mother waited in the inspector's office while High Wizard Vey was transferred to the larger interview room. Thordric stayed with them and made tea, telling them all about the other wizards he'd spoken to and how they'd reacted to the news of Kalljard's plot. Lizzie laughed when he told them about how he had dealt with Wizard Rarn and complimented him on his use of levitation.

A constable tapped on the door and told them the inspector was ready. Still laughing, they made their way downstairs.

The inspector showed them into the room where Vey sat waiting. 'Ladies, this is High Wizard Vey. High Wizard Vey, you've already met my pathologist, Maggie, and this is my sister, Lizzie.'

'Lovely to see you again, High Wizard Vey,' Thordric's mother said, sitting down.

'Yes, a pleasure...' Lizzie began, and then stopped dead, her breath caught in her chest. She gaped at Vey; he gaped back, equally shocked.

'What's the matter, Lizzie?' Thordric asked, glancing between her and Vey.

'He-he's my son,' she said.

19

THE TRUTH

The room was silent. Everyone was looking at Lizzie and Vey in utter disbelief. Vey stood up and walked around his side of the room. His usually calm face was screwed up in anguish, and he stopped and opened his mouth several times but nothing came out.

Thordric broke the silence, curiosity and concern fuelling him to speak. 'Is it true, Vey?' he asked quietly. Vey stopped and met his gaze, then silently gave a slight incline of his head, his tears splashing to the floor.

'I-I would never have known,' the inspector said. 'My own nephew! I didn't even recognise you.'

'That was the point, Uncle. I thought that if you couldn't recognise me, then it was unlikely mother would either,' Vey said, his voice trembling slightly.

'You thought that I wouldn't recognise you?' Lizzie said. 'I know it's been many years, Eric, but I would have recognised you even if it'd been fifty years, or a hundred. You are my son, and a mother always knows her son.'

'Even when he uses magic to try and grow his hair and ends

up looking like some kind of witless monster,' Thordric's mother said, trying to lighten the mood. She shot Thordric a glance and he grinned, while the inspector raised an eyebrow at him. But neither Lizzie nor Vey seemed to have heard.

'Why did you run, Eric?' Lizzie asked softly, her eyes wet. She walked closer to him, but he stepped back slightly.

'I had to, mother,' Vey said. 'You know what they did to father. I had to get them back.'

'But didn't you realise how dangerous that was? If they killed your father, didn't it cross your mind that they might have done the same to you?'

'It wasn't dangerous, mother. They didn't even know about me. How do you think I got into the council in the first place?' Vey said.

'I have no idea, Eric, why don't you tell us?' she said, her voice hardening. The inspector decided it was time to cut in.

'Lizzie, let's all go upstairs. I'll have some tea made and we can all sit down and talk about this in a civilised manner,' he said. He strode over to the door and held it open for them to walk through. Thordric's mother went first, taking Lizzie by the arm and leading her out. The inspector escorted them up, leaving Thordric to walk with Vey. He kept silent, unsure of what to say, but it was Vey who spoke up.

'My mother taught you how to use your magic, didn't she?' he asked, but it was more of a statement than a question. 'She's a good teacher. You must be a fast learner too, to have reached the level you're at and still be so young.'

'Sh-she told me about you,' Thordric blurted. 'How you ran away after your father died. We found your flute and his diary of magic in the safe at the end of the house.'

'I see. I didn't think she would take anyone up to that house once I'd gone, least of all someone with as much magic as you have. So, you broke the illusion then?'

'Yes. She'd just been teaching me how to make them to help with the case. When I looked at the safe properly, I knew something wasn't right about it. I had to try and lift it.' Thordric felt slightly embarrassed. 'I didn't mean to go through your private things.'

They went into the inspector's office, but Thordric was sent back out again to make tea and bring in Jaffa cakes. He tried to listen to what was being said, but all he could hear was a soft sobbing. When he went back in, the enormous pile of Jaffa cakes wobbling dangerously on the tray, he found them all silent and staring at each other. He quickly served them tea and then sat down in the chair nearest the door.

'So, Eric,' Lizzie said at long last, her voice harder than any of the ice freezing up the streets outside. 'Why don't you explain how you became part of the council?'

Vey took a large gulp of tea and ate one of the Jaffa cakes before speaking. 'When I ran away, I went straight to the Wizard Council Training Facility. I made up a story about having been in a coma since I was a child and that I had just discovered I had magical powers. I told them no one else in the family had ever had magic and, as everyone knows, only full wizards can come from families with no previous magic, so they believed me. They started me off with the basics, but I already knew most of the magic they were teaching and so I soon caught up with the others my age.'

'But you never gave any signs of having magic, even when your father tried to teach you,' Lizzie said. Her hair had fallen out of place again and now cascaded around her shoulders, but she took no notice.

'I'd known I had powers since I was a toddler. I accidently turned one of the Watchem Watchems into a tree once, although I was in such a panic about it that I somehow turned it back. It wasn't terribly happy with me, as I recall. Kicked me in the shin. Anyway, I didn't tell you or father about it because I didn't want to be a wizard, full or half. All I wanted was to be normal, but father believed in me regardless and so I used to practice the magic he tried to teach me at night so you wouldn't know.' He took another gulp of tea. 'Then after...after *it* happened, I found his diary and I knew that Kalljard had done it somehow.'

'You joined the council so that you could challenge him?' the inspector asked.

'That's how it started out, yes. But the more I learnt about him and about the council, the more I knew that something so childish wouldn't have been what father wanted. I began making plans to try and change the way the council thought instead.'

Lizzie took in a deep breath. 'Ten years I searched for you, Eric. Ten years I made myself sick with worry, not knowing whether you were dead or alive until my heart and my mind couldn't take it any longer. I stopped looking because it was too painful, and since then I've been trying to rebuild my life. And now I find you, I-I have no words.'

'I'm sorry, mother. I truly am,' Vey said. Thordric looked into his eyes and saw that he meant it. 'I wanted to contact you, so many times. I started to write letters, but it was no good. I couldn't risk them finding out who I really was. My cause was too important for that.'

Lizzie began to sob silently, and Thordric's mother gave her a handkerchief to dry her eyes with. Vey started to sob too, and soon even the inspector had great tears dropping off his nose to land in his moustache. Thordric shifted uncomfortably, feeling very much the outsider on what was now a family reunion. Then a thought struck him.

'Vey,' he said, now oblivious to the tears. 'Rarn told me something when I interrogated him that I have to ask you about.' His mother shot him a contemptuous look, but Vey looked up at him almost glad of the interruption.

'What was it, Thordric?' he said.

'He-he told me that you mixed the potion Kalljard wanted the council members to always drink,' Thordric said.

Vey straightened up, wiping the last of the tears from his eyes. 'Yes, Thordric, I did. He told me what the ingredients were and said I was to fill six cauldrons full of it a week. He made me drink a cupful first, so I wouldn't question his wishes. I managed not to drink it again, but the wizards always asked for it and so I carried on making it. I never realised the full effect that it had.'

'So, he ensnared you as much as everyone else,' Thordric said.

'I'm sorry to say he did,' Vey said sadly.

'This idea of yours, to change the way the council thinks, exactly how were you planning to go about it?' the inspector asked, wringing the tears out of his moustache.

'I wanted to get close to Kalljard, to find out how he thought and what motivated him. I thought that if I could do that, then I could find out why he had father killed and, the closer I would be to Kalljard, the more the council would trust me. I wanted to make it seem as though Kalljard was having a change of heart and was beginning to see that half-wizards are every bit as capable of magic as full wizards are.'

'And did you get close to him?'

'Yes, moderately so, but he didn't seem to trust me as much as he trusted Rarn,' Vey replied.

'Perhaps he figured out what you were up to,' Thordric said. He got out the paper detailing Kalljard's plot. 'We found this on Kalljard's desk. It had a pretty strong illusion spell on it, and so far, only Rarn has given away that he'd seen it before. I'm convinced that none of the other Wizards knew anything about it.' He held it out for Vey to look at. Vey read it and his face hardened. 'I have to ask you, Vey. Did you know about this?'

Thordric already knew the answer, but he had to let the others hear it. Vey looked at him. 'I did,' he said quietly.

They all stared: the inspector, his brow furrowed and his moustache curling; Lizzie, her eyes strong but damp; Thordric's mother, her eyebrows arched with intense curiosity.

'That wasn't all we found in Kalljard's room. There was a mirror, disguised as a wardrobe, and on the desk was a pot plant known as *Winsome Sunbeam.*'

'Or *Oppulus Nuvendor,* if you want to give it its technical name,' Vey interrupted. He sighed and looked at all the faces staring at him. 'You haven't missed anything, have you, Thordric? Yes, I knew about the plant and the mirror.'

'Would you like me to tell them what happened, or are you going to tell the story yourself?' Thordric asked, offering Vey some more Jaffa cakes. Vey took a handful and ate them all in quick succession.

'I'll tell them,' he said, hiccoughing. He stood up and paced around the office, trying to find the words. His heavy robes rustled with each step. 'Rarn, who normally cleaned Kalljard's chambers, was ill, so Kalljard asked me to do it instead. He said he wanted his mirror moved and to be replaced with a wardrobe that was to arrive that day. He then left, allowing me to snoop around. That's when I saw what he was planning and it made my blood freeze. Everything I was trying to achieve was meaningless after I saw it. He was willing to put thousands – and there truly are thousands – of half-wizards to death. I couldn't let that happen.'

He stopped, taking a deep breath, and ate some more Jaffa cakes. His hands shook slightly. 'I understand how you felt,

Vey,' Thordric said, trying to ease the High Wizard's conscience. Vey nodded appreciatively and carried on.

'I switched the mirror with the wardrobe as he'd asked, but I kept the mirror stored nearby so that I could put my hands on it if I needed to. Rarn had given Kalljard the plant as a gift the day before, though I doubt that worm knows what its properties are. I took a cutting from it and spent the next two days grinding it down and making it into a liquid. Then I put the mirror back in the room while Kalljard was out and waited for him to come back for his afternoon tea. I managed to stop Rarn from coming in by telling him that Kalljard had requested he iron his ceremonial robes. As no one else was allowed in, I knew I wouldn't be discovered.

'When Kalljard finally did walk in, I pretended I had only gone in to lay out his tea and sandwiches. I thought it was a rather weak excuse to be honest, but he seemed to believe it. Anyway, he ignored me and went to trim his beard. He noticed the mirror then, but I had already injected him with the *Winsome Sunbeam* by use of a magic dart.'

'A magic dart?' Thordric asked.

'Yes,' Vey said, now smiling. 'I came up with it myself. All you have to do is trap whatever liquid you have inside a sort of force field, which allows you to throw it from a distance and leaves no trace afterwards.'

'But we found a puncture mark on Kalljard's head, covered by the brown mark,' Thordric objected.

'*Almost* no trace, then,' Vey said. 'Either way, it had the desired effect. Within minutes he was hallucinating so badly that he thought his own reflection was a monster and tried to cast it away using a defensive spell. In his drugged state it rebounded, and caused his skin to harden like leather. It wasn't exactly what I'd planned, but I knew it would put him out of action long enough for me to destroy his plans and to reorganise the council.'

'But you didn't know it would react with his potion, did you?' Thordric's mother said, crossing her legs. Her red high heels glinted in the light.

'No, ma'am, I didn't,' Vey said. He sat down heavily in the chair and hung his head. 'I didn't mean for it to kill him, I simply wanted him out of the way for a while so I could make things right.'

Lizzie dried her eyes and stood up. Vey drew back, thinking she would rebuke him for what he'd done. Instead, she knelt beside him and took his hands. 'It wasn't your fault, Eric. Kalljard was a vile, evil man. The world is much better off without him,' she said gently. Everyone in the room murmured in agreement with her, and Vey looked at them gratefully. 'Carry on, Eric, and tell us what happened next,' she said.

Vey cleared his throat. 'Well...the potion reacted within minutes and when I looked at him and discovered he was dead, I panicked. I laid him on the bed so it looked like he'd simply died while taking a nap and I cast the strongest illusion I could over his plans so no one would suspect any foul play. I covered up the puncture mark, and then did the same with the mirror, but I heard footsteps near the door and had to rush. The illusion held, but only just. Then I stood behind the door so that I could slip out after whoever it was had entered. As it was, it was Rarn coming back, and as soon as he saw the body he yelled for help. I doubled back through the door to see what was going on.'

20

DECORATING THE STATION HOUSE

The inspector sent Rarn back to the council, laden with an official report declaring that High Wizard Kalljard's death had been an unfortunate accident, not murder. No one was to be blamed for it, and High Wizard Vey would be on leave for a week due to the stress the investigation had caused him. Apologies were given to all the wizards detained.

Thordric thought that letting Rarn go back to the council was far more than he deserved, considering his indifference to Kalljard's plans. He would have had him locked up for life, but as the inspector said, it was for Vey to decide what to do with him.

As for Vey himself, everyone in the inspector's office had unanimously agreed that he should be left to go free. In their eyes, he had acted accordingly for the good of the people, even if they didn't know it and, if it'd been possible, the inspector would have had him commended for it. This cheered Vey up dramatically. With his calm demeanour having returned, he made the withered rose on the inspector's desk return to full bloom.

'Mother,' Vey said to Lizzie. 'I know I never wrote, or let you know I was alive even, but...'

Lizzie put up her hand to silence him. 'Come home for a week, Eric. You look like you could use a decent meal.'

Vey agreed and turned to Thordric. 'If my uncle doesn't need you, I would like to invite you back for dinner. There's something I need to discuss with you.'

'And the snow in my garden needs melting again, boy,' Lizzie said, trying to keep a straight face.

Thordric and Vey spent the rest of the day at Lizzie's, since the inspector had let him leave after lunch.

They melted all the snow in both the front and back gardens and then Lizzie sent them upstairs to finish painting the room she and Thordric had started. Vey frowned at the colours she'd chosen, but he didn't dare suggest they were too bright. With both of them at it, it took barely fifteen minutes.

Of course, as Thordric had already found out, Lizzie always had more work to be done. She directed them up to the loft to clean, and when they got there, Thordric coughed in distaste. It was thick with dust, and cobwebs loomed mere inches above their heads.

'Where shall we start?' Vey began, but his eyes caught a large stack of books in front of him. 'These...these are my father's. I'd forgotten all about them.'

'Really? What are they about?' Thordric asked excitedly, his eyes lighting up.

'I believe,' Vey said, picking one of the books up and swiping off the dust, 'that they're more books on the potions he created, and properties of plants found around the town and near the river.' He waved his hand slightly and cleared all the dust from the rest of the books and the floor around them, before sitting down to read.

Thordric waited a moment, wondering if he would get back up to start working, but it was clear he was lost deep within the pages. Sighing, Thordric levitated him upside down and Vey dropped the book in surprise.

'What *are* you doing?' he demanded, hastily holding his robes up so that his underclothes wouldn't show.

'Your mother won't be happy if we don't clean up here,' Thordric said, absently spinning Vey around.

Vey looked at him guiltily. 'Oh, yes...the cleaning...'

Three hours later and, after Thordric had had to levitate Vey another five times, they finally finished cleaning the loft. It looked unrecognisable; everything was visible and stacked in orderly piles, and they could now see that the walls were as brightly decorated as the room they'd been painting earlier. They had even found more of Lizzie's husband's work, and with Vey laden down with as many books and scrolls as he could carry, they made their way downstairs to the kitchen.

The smell of Lizzie's cooking wafted through the corridor and after the stress of the morning, they found they were ravenous. They were about to sit at the table when she turned to them. 'May I ask what you two think you're doing?'

'We're simply sitting down for dinner,' Vey said, putting all the books and scrolls on the table. Lizzie arched her eyebrow so high that it seemed to merge with her hairline. Thordric caught the danger they were in immediately.

'Uh, actually, we were going to put all these things away and then scrub up. We wouldn't want to sit down at the table still covered in dust, would we, Vey?' he said, hastily picking the books back up and nudging Vey to do the same. Lizzie smiled and watched them run out the room. When they returned, she looked them over, nodding her approval, and only then did she finally serve their food.

Great slabs of chicken, ham, beef and turkey were piled onto Thordric's plate, as well as stacks of vegetables and potatoes. Vey dug in too and for a moment they were both too busy eating to talk about anything.

Thordric swallowed his last potato and took a swig of the fruit water by his plate. 'What was it you wanted to talk about?' he asked Vey.

Vey wiped his mouth with a cloth and Lizzie watched him with amusement. 'I wondered how serious you are about your magic,' he said.

Thordric shrugged. 'More serious than I've ever been about anything else. I would never have believed the things I can do now.'

'So, you would be willing to learn more?' Vey said, trying to cut through his own stack of meat.

'Of course I would. You were going to teach me more anyway, weren't you, Lizzie?' he said, turning to her.

'Yes, boy, I was. What is it you want with him, Eric?' she asked.

Vey grinned. 'I wondered if you would like to join the council, Thordric.'

Thordric stared at him. 'Are...are you serious?'

'Of course. I'll have to assert my authority a bit to make the other wizards accept you, but once you've joined, they would be able to see the abilities that half-wizards can have. That should sway their thinking to my plan.'

'I-I don't know what to say. I've never liked the Wizard Council. I suppose I've grown so used to them despising our type that it would be strange if I joined them,' Thordric said.

'I understand. It will be different though, now that Kalljard isn't around to spread his lies. I want to make the council better, Thordric. Not just in how they think but in what they do.' He looked Thordric in the eye. 'I need your help to do it. You've studied my father's way of magic, and the potions and spells he made. I mean to implement them within the council, so that we can *really* help people, instead of giving them gimmicks.'

Thordric laughed at that. 'My mother might not like you for that, she buys their special tea and coffee blends all the time – and their bath powder, come to think of it.' He thought for a moment. 'If it really is going to change...then yes, I would love to join the council.'

'Excellent. Now I don't know how long it will take me to straighten everything out when I get back after this week, so you might be stuck with my uncle for a bit longer,' Vey said, rather apologetically.

'He's alright, really,' Thordric said. 'Well, he is now that I grew his moustache back for him.'

They all chuckled, and Lizzie stacked up their now empty plates and went to get dessert. She came back with one of her cakes, only it was much larger than any Thordric had seen her make before and was stuffed full of chocolate sauce and cherries. He helped himself to a large slice, using his magic to direct the knife as he cut it. Vey watched him, an appreciative smirk touching his lips.

'I have a feeling he might not stay solely my boss for long,' Thordric continued. 'Judging by the way he and mother look at each other.'

'Yes, I noticed that,' Lizzie said, not altogether approvingly. 'Glancing at each other like youngsters no older than you, it's enough to make me come over faint sometimes.'

'I'm glad I'm not the only one,' Thordric grinned. He cut her and Vey large slices of cake too, and levitated them onto their plates. He rather enjoyed being able to do that.

'How good are your other magic skills, Thordric?' Vey asked, watching him. Thordric opened his mouth, but Lizzie cut across him.

'He figured out that wooden man your father took three weeks on in just two days. He has enough skill for anything you want of him, I'm sure of that,' she said, beaming. 'He can paint murals as well, and the Watchem Watchems seem to like him.'

Vey raised his eyebrows at this and tried to speak with his mouth full of cake. A sort of muffled grumbling came out and Thordric snorted at him. 'You saw the Watchem Watchems?' Vey said, swallowing. Thordric gave a modest shrug and told him all about his time in the woods with them. 'That's very impressive. Father said they only really like people with a kind heart...and very strong magic.'

The next day was unusual for Thordric, now that the investigation was over. He left for the station at the normal time, although he arrived slightly later than usual because he had to clear the street of snow again, for it had fallen heavily during the night.

Wondering what the inspector was going to ask of him now that his usefulness there had ended, he walked past all the constables at the desk, trying to nod and smile at them for all the help they'd given him lately. To his surprise, the inspector was glad to see him when he stepped into his office.

'Ah, there you are boy. I was about to go and ask your mother where you'd got to. Now that this whole messy wizard business is over, I was wondering if you would be up for doing a little job for me.'

Thordric raised his eyebrows. 'What is this job, Inspector?' he asked.

The inspector grinned, making his moustache dance about

in a most unusual way. It seemed to react to the inspector's happier moods now, as well as his irritated ones, and Thordric was highly suspicious that his magic had something to do with it. 'Take a look around you, boy,' the inspector said, gesturing around the station.

Thordric looked. The paint had started to peel in quite a few places, and that there was an unusual sort of moss growing in one corner. 'Starting to look a bit shabby, isn't it?' the inspector continued.

Thordric thought he knew where the inspector was heading. 'Would you like me to redecorate, Inspector?' he asked.

'Why yes, as a matter of fact I would,' he said. 'My sister happened to mention that lovely mural you did at her house near the woods. I thought we could use something like that here, to give the men some inspiration to improve their work ethic.'

Thordric thought it was a good idea. 'Is there anything specific you would like me to paint?'

The inspector thought for a moment, crinkling his moustache. 'Well, I think you levitating Wizard Rarn and forcing him to drink potion would look good, but I'll let you decide. I'm sure you can come up with something appropriate.' He flapped his hand at Thordric, signalling for him to go off and do it.

With a smile, Thordric surveyed the rest of the building, noting every crack and flake of plaster, every damp patch and every dent. With a single thought, he cleared away all the dust, dirt and moss, before heating the damp patches so that they dried out fully. The constables kept on stopping their work to gather around and watch him, but he didn't mind. He stripped off all the paint and replastered, smoothing over the walls so that he had a fresh canvas. Then, without paint or brush, he started his mural, making it large enough to fill the whole station.

Work had come to a complete stop by then. Even two constables, bringing in a thief they'd just caught, stood with their mouths agape, watching all the colours appear on the wall and take shape. Thordric carried on like that for the rest of the day, not even stopping to eat, for as he soon discovered, he could keep it going while doing other things.

The constable, who he had sent out in the snow two days before, even brought out a game of checkers and Thordric sat there playing a game with him while his painting casually continued by itself.

Unfortunately, the inspector came out of his office and saw them when they were only halfway through and took it away, sending all the constables lurking about out onto the streets to patrol. They grumbled unhappily as they went, putting on their winter jackets and boots as slowly as possible so they could watch the mural develop some more.

Night set in before Thordric was finished, but he stayed an extra few hours after everyone had gone to get it done.

When they walked in the next morning, none of them could speak.

The sight before them looked so real that all they could do was stare. Thordric had gone with the inspector's ideas about Rarn, but he had added in the constables bringing in the wizards and the ones that had stood on guard by the cells all night and by the interview rooms. Not a single man had been left out and Thordric grinned rather smugly as they all walked around the station identifying themselves on the wall.

'Why, you've outdone yourself there, boy!' the inspector exclaimed enthusiastically, clasping Thordric by the hand and giving it an almighty shake that almost wrenched his arm out the socket. His moustache was wet with tears that he hadn't managed to wipe away quick enough and his lower lip shook slightly with his bottled emotion. 'Lizzie told me about your arrangement with the High Wizard. I...we'll...you'll...you'll be missed, boy.'

'I've got at least another week left, Inspector,' Thordric pointed out. 'Besides, I'm sure my mother would be delighted to have you round for dinner now and then.' He grinned, seeing the inspector's face light up.

'She-she would?'

'Of course she would.'

'Well, in that case, er, boy...I have an errand for you to run.' He took Thordric into his office and handed him a note out of one of the drawers on his desk. 'Perhaps you could run down to the jeweller's when they open and give them this...you can spend the day at Lizzie's after that.'

Thordric took the note. not bothering to read what was on it because he knew already. He looked wryly at the inspector, but remained silent.

The jewellery shop was a short walk away and the snow had lessened considerably. When he got there the jeweller took the note without any questions, only a simple nod, and sent Thordric on his way.

He spent the rest of that day, and the rest of the week, pouring through Lizzie's husband's books with Vey. The ones on plants he found particularly interesting and he took regular walks around the town trying to find the winter herbs that were said to grow. Soon the week was up and Vey went back to the council. Thordric waited nervously for his summons, not knowing whether they would be the same afternoon or a month from then. He found he was excited.

21

A REVOLUTION

The sea of wizards looked on expectantly as Vey took to the platform.

He was dressed in silver-coloured robes and had the heavy mithril chain of his office strung about his neck, making him look slightly uncomfortable. Thordric stood to the side, wearing the cloak Lizzie had given him, trying to be as inconspicuous as possible. Even so, some of the wizards in the front row kept stealing glances at him.

He hoped they didn't recognise him from their time down at the station, for he had gone to a lot of trouble growing his hair down to his shoulders. He'd wanted a small goatee too, but his mother had argued with him for almost two hours over it, saying it made him look far too old, so he'd given up just to make her calm down.

He drew his attention back to Vey, who had already begun his speech. His voice echoed across the wide hall and even the deafest of wizards could hear it. The confidence in it made Thordric's own confidence rise, although his nervousness had him shaking slightly.

'Members of the council,' Vey said. 'Having now become fully affiliated with my position as High Wizard and after reviewing everything the council has achieved since its conception, it is time for me to reveal to you my plans for the improvement of our conduct and our offerings to the people.'

The crowd murmured at this, a mix of excitement and disapproval. Vey ignored it and carried on. 'Having discovered the foul plans that Kalljard wished to put into effect – and no, I will not dignify his memory with his title, for he does not deserve it – I wish to begin by changing our view of half-wizards.' He strolled down from the platform and walked along the rest of the stage, meeting them all with his strong gaze.

'After all,' he continued, 'what do we really know about them, truthfully?'

'Half-wizards claim they have magic, but everyone knows that is a lie,' one of the wizards near the stage shouted.

'No, they do have magic, but all they do is cause destruction,' another countered. Others joined in, and the babble grew so loud that Vey couldn't be heard over it. He held up his hands to quieten them and stood back up on the platform so that they could all see him. The hush soon spread throughout the crowd.

'I believe it is time for me to introduce our newest member.' He turned to Thordric, who was shaking so badly that his cloak quivered. 'Thordric, would you please step up here?'

Thordric tried to control himself and did as Vey said, taking in every look of suspicion that the other wizards gave him. Once he was up on the platform, Vey whispered something in his ear. Thordric listened attentively, trying to look calm and impressive.

Rolling up his sleeves, he raised his arms and focused on the walls of the chamber. Colours started spreading down them like a wave, creating swirls and patterns, and brightening the entire room. It spread up the pillars and onto the ceiling, across the floor and along the benches where the wizards were sitting. They watched with their mouths agape and touched the colours now surrounding them, exclaiming with incredulity when they didn't come off on their fingers.

Thordric's magic didn't stop there, however. The gargoyles along the ceiling jumped into animation, spreading their wings to fly about the room, dive-bombing the heads of the wizards. Wizard Rarn, who had been kept on solely as cleaner, had one chase him out of the room. Everyone could hear his screams echoing back along the corridor. Vey had taught Thordric that trick himself. It was a simple extension of the spell he'd used to make the wooden man come to life. This was the first time he'd used it properly and was greatly enjoying the results.

Out the corner of his eye, he saw Vey make a quick motion with his hand: time to finish the display. Thordric pulled his hands in and the colours drained from the walls to merge into a giant puddle on the floor. He flicked at it and the puddle dried to a multi-coloured powder that floated into the great fire grate at the back of the room. The gargoyles returned to their positions and became immobile once again, all except for the one chasing Rarn. Thordric felt it should stay animate for a while longer, purely for good measure.

He shrugged his sleeves back down his arms and stepped aside to let Vey carry on. Every wizard in the room was silent.

'As you can see, Thordric here has quite the talent, and I assure you it extends beyond simple tricks,' Vey said. The wizards all swallowed at that; every one of them knew what Thordric'd demonstrated was *not* simple by any means. 'At just under fifteen, he is also the youngest member ever to be on the council.'

'The council isn't here to babysit! He should still be in training at that age,' one of the middle-aged wizards shouted, clearly offended that someone so young would be allowed to join. There were murmurs of agreement from the surrounding wizards.

'But surely you can see, Wizard Ayek, that the Training Facility could offer him no further instruction?' Vey said. He was looking at the man as though he were an imbecile and Thordric chuckled silently. Wizard Ayek muttered something unintelligible.

'That is not all that will surprise you about young Thordric here,' Vey continued, pausing to survey the crowd. They were looking up at him, full of apprehension. 'He is also...a half-wizard.'

Cries of outrage echoed from all sides of the room, but were soon drowned by those of awe and deep revelation. Some of the wizards even stood up and applauded and Vey pushed Thordric forwards so that he could take a bow. Thordric breathed in deeply and bent over, closing his eyes with relief. He had expected them to react with anger, not applause.

'My good members of the council,' Vey said, his excitement coming out through his voice. 'We are now in a new age, an age where full wizards and half-wizards will be able to train together. We can stop this prejudice, for as you have witnessed, there is truly no reason for it. Half-wizards have been known to fail at magic, yes. But ask yourselves this: if you had no magical training, would you not fail also? Thordric here was trained by my own mother, who learnt to teach the ways of magic from watching my father, a half-wizard, who put himself in danger trying to focus and control his magic.'

The wizard who had interrupted earlier, Ayek, jumped up out of his seat. 'You? Our own High Wizard, are nothing but a-a *half*-wizard? This is outrageous!' He turned desperately to his brethren. 'We have to have another election! Only a full wizard can be High Wizard! If Kalljard had known...'

'He would have murdered me like he murdered my father,'

Vey said coolly. He seemed completely unconcerned by what he'd revealed and Thordric found he was worried for him.

The wizards around Ayek turned to him angrily. 'Shut up, Ayek, you idiot!' one of them said. Thordric looked at him and realised it was Wizard Batsu, the young wizard who'd helped Thordric at the morgue. 'Hasn't his reverence just shown you that it makes no difference whether he is a full wizard or half? Thordric's magic was more than equal to our own, and I don't recall you ever putting on a display like that!'

More and more wizards joined in and Thordric watched them all in disbelief. This was the Wizard Council, made up entirely of full wizards, who only hours ago had despised half-wizards, and now were...praising him?

Vey put his hands up again and called for silence. 'I know this revelation has unnerved some of you and those who feel I do not deserve to be High Wizard have every right to leave. Go and be free from the council, and the new beginning I shall be giving it.' Several wizards stood up to go.

'Know this, though,' Vey continued, watching them. 'I shall be keeping a very close watch on your activities and if any of you begin to do anything I feel inappropriate, dangerous, or illegal, then I will not hesitate to alert the authorities and make sure you are imprisoned for life.'

Thordric watched with satisfaction as the wizards sat down again, and Vey began to tell them of all the other plans he had for the council. A space was made in the front row for Thordric to sit among them and he did so happily.

That evening, when Vey had retired to his chambers, he summoned Thordric there to have supper with him. 'What did you think of my speech?' he asked as Thordric sat down.

'To be honest, Vey, you scared the wits out of me. I thought they would all revolt against you and carry both of us out of the hall and lock us up for life!'

Vey chuckled. 'That's exactly why I needed you there,' he said, drinking some juice made from the strange fruit that grew in the council gardens. 'Say, whatever happened to that gargoyle you set on Rarn?'

Thordric blinked. 'I think it might still be chasing him,' he said, slightly nervously. Vey roared with laughter, almost missing the knock at the door.

'Come,' he said, waving his hand so it opened. Wizard Batsu appeared in the doorway, carrying a tray with a plate of Jaffa cakes and a note on it.

'Excuse me, your reverence. Wizard Thordric,' he said, nodding to them and putting the tray down on the table. 'This letter has just arrived for you.' Vey thanked him and watched him leave before picking up the note to read it.

'It seems your theory about your mother and my uncle was right, Thordric,' he said with a smile. 'We've been invited to their wedding.'

Dear reader,

We hope you enjoyed reading *Unofficial Detective*. Please take a moment to leave a review, even if it's a short one. Your opinion is important to us.

Discover more books by Kathryn Wells at https://www.nextchapter.pub/authors/kathryn-wells-fantasy-author

Want to know when one of our books is free or discounted? Join the newsletter at http://eepurl.com/bqqB3H

Best regards,
Kathryn Wells and the Next Chapter Team

The story continues in:
Accidental Archaeologist

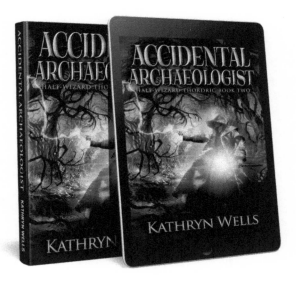

To read the first chapter for free, please head to:
https://www.nextchapter.pub/books/accidental-archaeologist-
middle-grade-fantasy-adventure

ABOUT THE AUTHOR

Kathryn Wells is the pen name of author Kathryn Rossati, a writer of fantasy, children's fiction, short stories and poetry.

As a child, she found her passion for the written word, and even though she had many other interests growing up, writing was always the one she would return to.

Her favourite authors are Diana Wynne Jones, Geanna Culbertson, Suzanne Collins, Jonathan Stroud, Neil Gaiman, Garth Nix, and David Eddings, to name but a few.

You can find more information about Kathryn on her website:

http://www.kathrynrossati.co.uk

BOOKS BY THE AUTHOR

Unofficial Detective (Half-Wizard Thordric Book 1)
Accidental Archaeologist (Half-Wizard Thordric Book 2)
Unseasoned Adventurer (Half-Wizard Thordric Book 3)
The Door Between Worlds

Unofficial Detective
ISBN: 978-4-86751-898-4

Published by
Next Chapter
1-60-20 Minami-Otsuka
170-0005 Toshima-Ku, Tokyo
+818035793528

12th July 2021

Lightning Source UK Ltd.
Milton Keynes UK
UKHW010026280721
387881UK00001B/173

9 784867 518984